COPOUT

COPOUT

by Bart Cline

UNDERSTATED PRODUCTIONS

For Eleanor

Published by Understated Productions 2013
www.copout.biz

Published in Great Britain
ISBN 978-0-9567787-2-7

Typeset in Minion Pro by Understated Productions
Printed by CreateSpace

Contents

Acknowlegements

I would like to thank a few people who have made a difference to this book in one way or another.

Casey Case, my screenwriting teacher in the late eighties, for casting his eye over Copout at several stages and offering helpful suggestions.

Doug Johnstone, a fellow writer, who also offered useful advice concerning the story.

Dan Flowers, Jeanie Flowers, Erin Oliver, Patrick Fraser, and assorted other friends who have read, listened, and commented.

My wife Eleanor, for supporting me all the way through the writing process, and my writing career so far, and to whom this book is dedicated.

And thank you, reader, for reading.

Bart Cline
England 2013

Chapter 1 – Cop

Only your armed response vehicle's headlights lend any definition to the ramshackle neighbourhood you're driving through. The flashing lights atop the police car cast eerie shadows in every other direction as you speed down the street. The setting could almost be unreal—your vision is tinged with tiredness, while your mood is reflected in the darkness with its writhing phantoms limned in red and blue. But without doubt it is real. Your dreams are never this ugly.

It's not even a neighbourhood. It's a derelict swarm of obsolete architecture that lends your city a black heart. This place gives the most desperate criminals a place to hide. A labyrinth of disused and unwanted edifices, the whole area should have been knocked down decades ago, and but for the efforts of the "Sites of Historic Interest" crowd it would have been.

Your partner sits quietly next to you as your car hurtles through the abandoned city, which begins to look not so abandoned. One of your colleagues, a man whose name you don't know, stands on patrol outside one of the crumbling brick and cement structures. He is helmeted, decked out in body armour, and armed. He holds his automatic weapon like a second shield across his chest. The grim expression on his face betrays the standard feeling that any of you experience when entering the Outlands, as the former industrial centre is now nicknamed. It may have been better in the past, but now nobody comes here except the violent and, today, the cops. The layout and structure of the buildings is so dense that the area defies any attempt to light it at night.

Slowing down as you near your destination, you see several other police officers similarly equipped and patrolling. All carrying the same burden of dread, these uniformed

9

constables are normally full of confidence that they will always get their man.

You take your eyes off the road long enough to sneak a glance at your fatigued visage in the rearview mirror, noticing the tired shadows under your eyes. Fortunately, your uniform is smart, giving the proper impression of one of Her Majesty's police inspectors. Despite the minimalism of today's police uniforms many of the other officers manage, as the working day lengthens, to look as rumpled as Columbo.

Always clean-shaven and well-turned out, you represent the force well. (Never mind how well the force represents you—or not.) Although your uniform is a good ambassador for the force, you're not always aware of the effect your face has. Like your last name, your face could be stone. Your features are chiselled and hard, and the lines of stress, loss, and premature ageing etch your skin, complementing your weary eyes.

Chief Inspector Hudson waves his arms to get your attention as you approach, having kept an eye on your car from some distance away. He is one of the rumpled Columbos, but he has seniority over you, so you bear with him. Try as you might, his personality resists your efforts to disrespect him.

You bring the car to a nevertheless disrespectful stop scant inches away from him, but he doesn't flinch. He never does, and that's why you respect him—or rather don't disrespect him. You used to call him a friend.

You kill the engine and exit the car, but Hudson says, "Hey Don," before you even close the door. The Chief Inspector looks tired and drawn as well, although he's older than you so he's got just as much of an excuse. But he looks generally more sympathetic and softer than you do. People like him better too. People used to like you. Hudson wasn't your only friend. A barbecue or a trip to the pub with your colleagues wasn't out of the question, and sometimes you even extended a kindness to them. They knew you as, if not someone to talk to and confide in, a reliable partner.

Your partner is also out of the vehicle and on his feet but, as usual, he gets away from you as soon as he can, conversing and learning what he can from the other more forthcoming cops nearby.

Glancing around, you notice several more armed and armoured men standing around an open manhole, pointing their automatic rifles down into it. You notice their safeties are off, and trigger fingers are ready. Had they even paid attention in their firearm safety courses?

Hudson is also wearing body armour, but he holds only a pistol in his hand, his automatic weapon slung over his shoulder. His body language screams caution, but directed at you personally rather than the situation.

The uniformed constables standing over the manhole are looking jumpy, their fingers hovering over the triggers, sweat dripping from their chins.

"Where are they?" you say to Hudson.

The chief inspector only gestures with his pistol toward the manhole, keeping his eyes trained on it for a moment as if wondering if he had seen something.

"Do they have any hostages?" you ask.

Hudson turns back to you and shakes his head. "No. We saw them go down about an hour ago, and nobody's seen them come out. We've got a few men knee-deep in the muck down there, but they haven't found anything yet."

A gesture from Hudson directs your attention to a vintage utility van, probably of Second World War provenance, in good condition, abandoned and positioned in such a way as to partly block the road. It has no registration plates, and all its doors stand open. You look inside it and underneath, seeing nothing else suspicious.

A couple more manholes are visible from where you're standing, their dark bowels reluctant to offer up the secrets they harbour. The cops standing over them are trying to get a look down below by probing with infrared cameras and microphones deep into the holes on long booms. They are doing a good job of penetrating the subterranean darkness with their high-tech gadgets, but without finding what they are looking for.

What you and they cannot see is a gutted brick and concrete hut not that far away from you. It is so decrepit that it could collapse at any moment. You also can't see the torch lights flickering from the rough hole dug into the floor, nor hear the faint tap of boots on metal rungs. None of you can. The lights are moving about rapidly as they rise higher and nearer to the ground, until their owners turn them off. The sounds rise as well, and nobody is near enough to hear them.

As you are discussing the situation with Hudson, your briefing is rudely interrupted.

A woman runs from one of the nearby buildings. She shouldn't be here—nobody should. She wears raggy clothes and tousled hair, with wild eyes and a nose once broken and unrepaired. Panic is visible on her face as she approaches you and Hudson.

"What's going on?" she shrieks. "Why does everybody have guns?" Her eyes dart around, wide and inquiring, taking in the scene from her probably distorted and crazed perspective.

Speechless, all you can say is, "What the hell...," and even that is an effort. You're not interested in why she should happen to be here, in a condemned area, skulking around in buildings overdue for the wrecking ball, and under a police lockdown to boot. To your credit, you think only of her safety. Crazy squatter though she may be, you do have a duty of care.

"This place ain't no shootin' gallery! G'way! I ain't done nothin' wrong!" Even as she continues her excitable jabbering, you grab her by the wrist and force her to your car. She resists. "Watch where you're puttin' them hands!"

"Perhaps you'd prefer to stay in the open when the firing starts," you say. "But you might get in the way of a bullet, and I'd get blamed." Opening the back door, you shove the woman into the back seat with no thought for her personal comfort, and then you get in with her, making sure she doesn't leave.

"Get your meat hooks off me! Leave me alone! Brute!" She struggles and squirms, but thankfully makes no attempt to exit the car.

Making eye contact with her, you gather the power of command in your voice. "Shut up!" You will the words into her eyes and brain. You need to be able to focus on the job you came to do.

As you take your Glock 17 pistol from its holster strapped to your thigh, she complies, bringing her knees up to her nose and wrapping her bony arms around her legs. You flick the magazine out of your weapon to check it while the woman looks all around with darting eyes, taking in the scene in the false safety of the car. Nerves showing with every breath and quiver, her eyes alight on your fully loaded ammunition clip, and this time she stares you down as a moment of understanding passes between you. Does she expect to survive? Does she know you will do what you can to protect her?

Examining the sidearm that you are rarely allowed to carry, you see that its clip is full, and you press it home into the grip with a heavy satisfying click. "Time to do some damage. You stay down," you say.

And then you hear the distinctive crack of automatic weapon fire.

It has started.

Your instinct for self-preservation tells you to duck, but as the defender of the innocent you need to know what's going on, so you guardedly bring your head up. You see one of your comrades-in-arms, a man you know as well as you know anybody on the force, fall to the ground, clutching his leg where a bullet has taken away a chunk of flesh. He is one of those men with whom you used to share beer and banter.

Looking away from your friend (if you could truly be said to have one) you see the dilapidated hut that you failed to notice previously. Three men sporting ski masks, more heavily armed than any of you, are emerging from the building, firing their weapons with extreme lack of prejudice. Each one carries a military grade automatic rifle, and pistols tucked into his belt. The ammunition bandoliers they wear are surely more of an affectation than of any practical use, except... The grenades attached to their clothing were of practical use—not army surplus toys, but modern tools of the trade any professional mercenary would be practiced with.

As the wounded officer writhes in agony on the ground, another constable runs to the rescue of his injured colleague, and takes a slug in his chest. The bullet passes straight through as if his flak jacket doesn't exist. Armour piercing rounds such as those aren't available to common criminals. But where these guys got their ammunition is not your problem right now. You would think the constable might be dead before he even falls across his injured friend but, no, he twitches and spasms before expiring, exhaling his last as the blood trickles down his chin.

You notice the crazy lady watching avidly through the rear window. "Get down!" you bark at the woman under your protection. You follow your own advice, pressing yourself down into the seat cushion, but she fails to act quickly enough. The report of gunfire deafens as a burst of bullets disintegrates your car's windows, showering you with pellets of glass.

The woman droops across you, her head wounds bleeding profusely on your uniform. You could beat yourself up about the fact you were supposed to be taking care of her, but she should have done as she was told—never mind that she shouldn't have been here to begin with.

Nevertheless, a shudder of horror tinged with regret goes through your spine, momentarily compromising your professionalism. Banishing the feeling, you push her off of you and prop her up against the opposite door. You are only trying to get her out of your way, not to give your enemies a target, but what else can you do? Gasping as the adrenaline grabs you, you raise your head to look out the window.

The gunmen are firing their weapons in the dark, not aiming very well. Their bullets impact everywhere, raining down chips of brick, shattering the remnants of already broken windows.

Maybe they don't know you're here. Maybe you have a chance. All your colleagues are out in the open.

You raise your gun.

You take aim, getting a good look at the ski masks, each of which sports a sewn-on badge over the forehead: Wolverines. Why does that seem familiar to you?

You fire.

Their ski masks provide no protection against a weapon such as your pistol. You would think they would wear helmets and body armour if they wanted to survive.

But if they wanted to survive, they wouldn't have started this rampage at all.

The perp in the centre drops, his brain severely impaired.

If they didn't know about you before, they do now, even if you've ducked again to stay out of their sight. It was worth it. You brought one of them down. Only two left.

The indiscriminate hail of bullets continues, and you hear some of the hot lead thud into your car. If you survive this, the car won't. Not that you care. It doesn't belong to you.

Adrenaline pours forth, practically coming out of your pores. Your breathing comes heavy and fast now, as if you just ran a mile in record time and then continued on to a triathlon without stopping to collect your medal.

Taking a few deep breaths, and keeping your head down low, you look out the window again, surveying the scene. The thugs are a bit closer, but they're taking their time as if there's no pressure at all.

You raise your gun, but now you're shaking too much to do anything with it. That's the problem with adrenaline. Fight or flight isn't good enough—you need to aim as well.

The remaining gunmen see you, and concentrate their fire in your direction making further mincemeat of the car. You squeeze yourself down as low as you possibly can as their bullets fly, trying to make yourself one with the seat cushion.

The door on your side is still open, and you chance a glance out. Your perspective through the car door is limited, but the ground seems littered with bodies. Either you're hallucinating—you sincerely wish you were—or you didn't know there were that many cops here backing you up. Hudson is taking cover behind a dilapidated wall, which fails to stop the bullets of the assassins. You see Hudson take a slug and go down. You wonder if he's still alive.

Meanwhile, the gunmen are still advancing. They are too close to you for comfort. Something has to be done. You must act quickly. Shaking gun hand or not, you lean out the door and fire at them until your clip is empty. It makes no difference—you wasted your bullets, not one of which connected with its target, scarcely qualifying as covering fire.

You pull back into the relative safety of the car, still untouched by injury. You can't help but be aware of the woman's lifeless body—put her out of your mind. You sneak another look at Hudson who, prone on the ground and soaked in blood, is engaging in a firefight with the gunmen. The wall behind which he had been taking cover is now mostly on top of him. At least it offers some protection. You catch a glimpse of one of the terrorists—or whatever they are—turning himself away from you and toward the fallen Chief Inspector. Those bricks and blocks covering him won't turn away very many bullets, nor last very long.

Your gun is empty. You need to fix that. You keep fresh magazines in one of the bulky compartments of your flak jacket. Still hunkering down out of the line of fire, your probing hand finds the clip, touching its cold metal.

But you can't close your fingers on the vital ammunition—your hands won't stay still. Fear and adrenaline has got them shaking as if the ambient temperature were below zero on this hot summer night. Concentrating, you succeed in grabbing the ammunition, and attempt to load your gun. The relentless shakes make it near-impossible.

Hurry! Come on… After a little eternity you get the clip fitted into your gun, and not a moment too soon. You are again ready for action, you hope.

You are lying on your back in the rear seat of the car, your head resting on the knees of the dead woman. At least she made herself useful for that much. Credit where it's due.

Lifting up your head for another look at the progress of your enemies, you see the gunman's hand holds a .44 magnum pistol, which will do terrible things to you if he gets a shot off. He's practically on top of you.

You lie back on the bench seat, looking up at the shattered rear window of your car as the gunman's hand probes into it, angling downward to point his weapon at you. You jam your foot into his wrist, crushing it against the beads of broken glass that still cling to the rim of the shattered window. Applying all the pressure you can, you hold him in place, dimly aware that he might at any moment bring up his other hand to spray you with automatic gunfire. Raising your head just enough to see his masked face, you give him everything you've got, emptying your gun into him point-blank while anchoring his hand with your foot. You continue pulling the trigger, only vaguely aware of the depleted clicking sound the weapon makes.

You release his wrist and he falls, thumping against the body of the car. There is no way this guy is getting up again.

Red encroaches at the edges of your vision. The world seems to be on a mad merry-go-round. Your chest is like a blast furnace. Fatigue grips you like a vacuum. You're shaking seemingly beyond any kind of control.

It isn't easy, but you release the gun from the iron grip of your hands and let it drop. The sound it makes as it hits the floor of your car is amplified twentyfold, as if you had not just endured the deafening sounds of impacts and close-quarters gunfire. Tumbling out onto your knees, you take in the full carnage as you get your feet under you and stand up. Your balance is shaky, and you sway like a graceless dancer.

Hudson must've taken down the last perp, even though you weren't aware of it at the time. He always was a tough nut. Hudson looks like he'll do okay with a little care and attention from a pretty nurse—probably just a broken rib or something—though he's unconscious now.

The cop with the injured leg is still alive. You hope he'll walk again soon.

A few other survivors can be heard coughing and grunting and groaning. You expected the body count to be high, but at a glance it looks like there are more survivors than casualties. As you steady yourself on your feet, you summon the paramedics and try to decide who to help first.

Chapter 2 – Business of Blood

Call me narcissistic, but I always liked standing at my fourth floor window and surveying my kingdom below. My subjects filled the street below my office in downtown Chicago.

A few floors above the hoi-polloi, anyone can be a king.

It was nineteen forty-something, eight o'clock at night, and the street was chock-a-block with Edsels, Studebakers, great big shiny Chevrolets, and other gas guzzling American cars jockeying for position. Traffic cops operating at every intersection did their peculiar dances. The hubbub of horns, bicycle bells, newsboys shouting "Extry! Extry! Read all about it!", and the click clack of heels in their thousands upon the sidewalks thundered up from street level.

The busyness would continue until late at night. It was a twenty-four-hour town. The male pedestrians all wore double-breasted suits and fedoras. High heels, elegant hats, and pencil thin skirts adorned the ladies. The children were dressed in oversized flat caps, suspenders, knee-length shorts, rolled-down socks, and scuffed black shoes.

People breathed, thought, digested, grew, and blood coursed through their veins in abundance.

The brass plaque at the front door of the building bore the bold inscription, "Donovan Stone Private Investigator".

If it hadn't been such a beautiful night I wouldn't have bothered coming into work at all. I felt lousy. But the bright summer moon beckoned me to come out.

My own house wasn't serviceable right now—more accurately, there was no such thing—and I had slept on the comfortable sofa in a former client's living room for the umpteenth time this year. His blackout curtains ensured I could sleep the sleep of the dead all day long.

I needed a shave, my clothes were rumpled from bedding down in them, and my two-tone shoes could have used a shine—but at least I was well-rested.

Some bats fluttered high above the street, gorging themselves on the bugs which nourished them and gave them the energy to fly. I would have liked to join them up in the air, dancing above the cares of the city, swooping down on the unsuspecting insects on the sidewalk below, free and well-fed.

But, back in the world of the living, I could pick out a particular rhythm of high heels on the sidewalk below making its way to the front door of my building, even among the flowing mass of warm bodies also clattering along down there.

The sound of her distinctive gait distinguished itself from the heels worn by the general class of heels down there. This was a woman of breeding. Her parents had no doubt sent her to a finishing school, probably in Europe—I guessed Switzerland. Her weight, about a hundred pounds. Shoes: Gucci. Her blood: hot. This was someone I would have liked to meet—someone who would have nothing to do with the downtrodden likes of me.

I heard the front door shut four floors below, so I moved away from the window, bored with the sounds of the street now that she was no longer a part of it.

I went to my desk and shoved the pile of junk onto the floor with a satisfying flutter of papers and shattering of coffee mug. My cleaning lady could take care of it later, whenever I got around to hiring one. Or my butler.

If I hadn't been at the office this particular evening I might have missed the most rewarding case of my career—if my work could be called a career thus far.

As I sat down in my old but comfortable executive chair I opened my "drinks cabinet". That's code for the bottom drawer of my desk, which contained a single bottle of Irish whiskey and a glass. It wasn't my preferred drink, but it was easier to come by than my actual favourite. I poured, ignoring the chip missing from the rim of my glass which, like the chair, was an old favourite.

I had no appointments today, but my office door opened anyway, revealing a fantasy, a vision. It was the woman whose shoes I had heard from the street. I was sure my heart had stopped. She looked even better than I had imagined, sporting full red lips and lengthened eyelashes. Her slender neck pulsed with smooth allurement. She ignited hungers which I spent most of my nights denying, or at least restraining. Beauty purer than any old statue or any new movie starlet. I couldn't take my eyes off her.

I felt the bottle in my hand. Forgetting I had already poured myself a drink, I poured another one and the liquor overflowed my glass onto my desk, already stained from other food and drink. It was far more than I could drink and remain standing, due to my haemoglobin deficiency.

"Good morning," I said, picking up some sheets of paper from the floor, and attempting and failing to blot up the spilled drink with them.

She paused as she took in my surroundings. Even in the low light the place was embarrassing.

Raising one eyebrow in rebuke, she said, "Drinking on the job?" Even disapproving, her voice was like a perfectly tuned musical instrument in the hand of a virtuoso, melodious even as she criticised me.

"I'm not feeling well right now," I said. "Can I help you?"

"If you're not feeling well," she trilled with addictive overtones, "perhaps I should come back tomorrow." The seams of her skirt emphasised the authoritative angle of her hips as she turned to leave.

I stood up, sending my chair crashing into the wall behind me, littering the floor with chunks of plaster.

"No no no, I'm feeling better by the second, really. Please, have a seat."

I motioned to a chair and she sat down, crossing her legs and showing a bit more stocking than was polite. I looked at her alluring eyes rather than her elegant legs.

"Thank you, Mr Stone."

"Please, call me Donovan, Miss…"

"Smith. You may call me Jessica." Excellent. A first-name rapport. I resisted the impulse to smile—she might not like my teeth.

"Jessica," I said, savouring the flavour of the name on my tongue. "Very well. Would you like a drink?"

"No, thank you."

"You don't mind if I have one, do you?" I raised my over-full glass slightly, only spilling a tiny amount. "I know your name from somewhere, don't I? Oh yeah, you're the daughter of John 'Frenchie' Smith, the most powerful man in Chicago's underworld until he was bumped off about a year ago. Running a city from below can earn you a few friends. But with friends like those… right?"

She spoke in a languid tone with the force of an unhasty river, hardly opening her mouth to allow the words out. "How do you know that, Mr Stone?" Back to 'Mr Stone'. Hmm.

Jessica took her hat off, and her silken hair fell like a stage curtain over her squared shoulders. But unlike an asbestos stage curtain, her hair fairly smouldered.

"Well, I didn't read it in the newspapers, doll. Your old man must have left you pretty well set up."

"I'm not hiring you to investigate me, Mr Stone," Jessica said.

"I said call me Donovan, and it's necessary for me to know something about my clients. I need to survey the lay of the land on both sides of the border. So what do you want me to investigate?"

Jessica rose from her chair. She paced up and down the office, looking at her fingernails. The tailored cling of her skirt hugged and flattered her rolling hips, and her feet cut through the clutter on the floor like an icebreaker. I took my glass, leaned back in my chair, and swung my feet on to the splash of liquor on my desk. The first sip of my whiskey tasted terrible, but I told myself it was good and that made it so.

"Last night, I got home and discovered that my apartment had been searched." Jessica seemed a little bit choked up over this. "It was just little things. A drawer left open, a few things slightly out of place. Just enough for me to notice."

"Was anything missing?"

"Not—" Choking back the tears, Jessica missed one. "I'm sorry Mr Stone. A man broke into my home, looked through my private things, and meant for me not to notice. And what if I hadn't noticed? He could do it again and again. He could be watching me everywhere I go, seeing me while I'm eating, sleeping, washing, dressing…"

"Don't worry about it, doll. You won't have to feel anybody's eyes on you for long. I've got your six. If anybody tries to hurt you, I'll be at his throat."

"Thank you Mr Stone," she said, dabbing her eyes with her handkerchief. "You inspire confidence." She shifted in her chair, returning to the subject. "No, nothing's missing. Not that I've been able to detect."

"I'll do the detecting, doll. Do you suspect anyone?"

"My former fiancé, Martin Zarkov, or possibly someone working for him."

"Why would he want to search your apartment?" Come on Donovan. A jilted fiancé harbouring a grudge… the possibilities are endless. "Never mind. Stupid question. I assume you want me to find out what in particular he's looking for."

"Yes. And put a stop to it if you can."

"I can investigate him. That's what I do. And I don't work cheap. I charge twenty five dollars a day, plus expenses. But to make him stop, now that's hard work…"

"I'll give you a bonus of five hundred dollars."

"… and I'm just the kind of guy to do it, doll. First thing I want to do is see your apartment."

"Really," she said, raising an eyebrow.

Jessica's apartment was decorated in a minimalist but sumptuous art deco style, all clean lines and tasteful shades of grey.

The living room sported a sofa, love seat, coffee table, and drinks cabinet. I was surprised the intruders could find anything to search. There was not a fleck of dust on any surface. The velvety sofa was brushed so all the fibres pointed the same direction. She obviously had a maid. The place was immaculate.

No, not quite immaculate. There were a few things out of place, just as Jessica had said. The square coasters on the coffee table were not quite angled in keeping with the meticulous tidiness of the place. I also spotted a single hair on the floor.

"Is this exactly how it was when you noticed something was wrong?"

"Yes, I haven't moved anything. Come, walk this way."

"If I could walk that way—"

"I didn't hire you as a humorist, Mr Stone," Jessica said.

"Good thing too—I can't remember the rest of that line."

Jessica led me into her bedroom. She almost floated rather than walked. If I could walk that way… I wouldn't need legs.

Decorated in the same style as the living room, the budoir gave her apartment unity. A dresser and mirror on one side, a wash basin on another side, a freestanding wardrobe, and a four-poster bed with a silk draped canopy. The kind of place where you'd never want to get out of bed.

"But I do usually charge extra to work in clients' bedrooms."

"Mr Stone—"

I held my hands up in mock apology.

Jessica kept her eye on me for a moment to make sure I understood that the silliness was to stop. "This is the drawer that was left open."

She glided into the en-suite bathroom.

"There was also a brush left on the counter in here, and a couple of dresses moved in the closet."

"I'm impressed with your organisational skill. I have enough trouble finding my toothbrush."

I looked at the things in the drawer that she had indicated, which was full of typical woman stuff: brushes, combs, compacts, rouge, several shades of lipstick. I'm sure if I had known what it looked like before the break-in I could have gleaned a wealth of information from its current state. But of course, a client only calls you in after something has happened.

"What do you think he was looking for?" I asked. "A confident girl like you should have at least some idea."

"Something he left here once, something of mine, something hidden here that I don't know about? He was a secretive man, and I don't think I ever knew what he was thinking. Your guess is as good as mine. Better, I hope. That's what you're here for. With your honed instincts, courage, finely tuned intellect, and keen eye, you should be able to crack this case wide open."

The silver tongued minx sure knew how to press the right buttons. Of course she was right, but how could she know it, having only just met me?

I took a few things out of the drawer—a brush, some silky undergarments, a lipstick—and examined them closely.

I was not very comfortable handling all that girly stuff, and I didn't know what I was looking for anyway. I dropped them back in the drawer and closed it.

"I might as well get to work now." I made for the door.

"What do you want me to do?" she asked, expectantly.

"Get on with your life," I said.

Grabbing my hat and buttoning up my coat, I left Jessica's apartment and closed the door behind me, relishing the prospect of getting stuck in. It was the best job I'd had in... well, a long time.

The next day was one of appalling sunshine and tiresome warmth.

My plan was to tail her so I could see who else was tailing her and tail him.

Crouching behind any available cover—dumpsters, trash cans, cars—I kept her in sight. I probably need not have bothered hiding, because all the people vying for their own little bit of the sidewalk as they went about their routine business of the day would have provided ample cover for an elephant. I wouldn't have stood out, even dressed the way I was—in my trench-coat, hat, gloves, and sunglasses—despite the baking heat. My collar was turned up. What can I say? I've got a low sun threshold.

At least the night would fall soon. The sun was low in the sky, and I did my best to keep it off my skin.

In the midst of this ever moving throng, I had not only to track Jessica, but to find her watcher, who without doubt would be trying as hard as I not to be found.

But I was the detective, and I spotted him.

This particular tail happened to be Dave, my former partner from ten years ago. When we went into business together, we had high hopes of cleaning up the city and making a lot of money to boot. After a while we dissolved the partnership because of our different methods of detecting.

Dave was across the street, laying low behind a paddy wagon, much closer to Jessica than I was. I was surprised she hadn't felt his breath on her neck. When she went into a shop I crossed over to approach Dave.

I was halfway across the street before he saw me and bolted away. Gaining the sidewalk, I played it smart instead of running after him at full pelt.

Dave's path would carry him directly in front of the First National Bank. A truck from Acme Security was parked in front of the bank, making a delivery. A very large safe was being hoisted up to the second floor using a rope and pulley system. The ropes were taut and stretching, already feeling the strain from the load which was must have weighed a couple of tonnes. Several brawny men were working the ropes, and others at the second-floor window to pull the safe in.

I drew a revolver from my shoulder holster, planted my feet solidly on the ground, held the gun in a careful grip, and took aim in the direction of the safe.

I had been a deadeye in the army, given my extraordinarily acute perception. This would be a pretty easy shot. I fired.

The rope broke and the safe fell directly in front of Dave. He was running so fast he couldn't stop as the now immovable object crunched into the ground in front of him and shattered the concrete of the sidewalk. The clang of his head against the metal safe rang out as he ran headlong into it and bounced off, falling backward to the ground dazed.

I sauntered over to Dave and picked him up by the necktie. He was too stunned to notice either the goose-egg growing on his forehead or the choking noose of his tie.

As I began to drag Dave away, the bank manager burst out of the front door of his venerable institution, livid. The veins protruding redly from his neck and temples almost glowed in the fading sunshine.

"Stone," the manager fumed as he examined the damaged safe and sidewalk, up and down and inside and out, "you're going to pay for the damage to that safe. It'll cost at least a hundred dollars." He looked down his nose at me with an authoritarian glint.

I gave him the full force of my gaze. I wasn't about to let him give me any guff. "Remember when your bank hired me to find a man who was going to rob the place?" Pitting my greater height against his greater girth, I poked him in the chest with my outstretched finger as I let my eyes bore into his. "If I hadn't caught him you might have lost everything. I seem to remember doing about a hundred dollars' worth of work on that case that I forgot to bill you for."

"A hundred dollars' work," he conceded, his eyes misty, "definitely."

Having overcome objections, I dragged Dave behind me by his neckwear, beating a hasty retreat from the bank.

Dave and I gained the back alley and I let go of his tie. Sprawling on his back, his trench coat soiled with the filth of the alley, Dave groaned and probed his forehead with his fingers. Breathing in sharply as he found the still growing lump, he made a somewhat unwilling effort to raise himself, rolling on to all fours before kneeling, and finally making a shaky but successful attempt to stand.

"You know, Dave," I said, "the lady, she doesn't like having her place searched."

"No, Don, it's enough to say 'the lady doesn't like having her place searched.' The 'she' is redundant."

I didn't get to be the best unknown detective in Chicago by losing my cool whenever I was provoked. I mentally pushed away the red that was encroaching on the edge of my vision.

"And me, I don't like having my grammar corrected," I said, congratulating myself on my restraint. "Now tell me, why are you tailing Miss Smith, what were you looking for in her apartment, and who are you working for? And if I don't like your answers—"

"You don't know?" Dave looked almost incredulous.

"I wouldn't be asking," I said, a little less confident than I had been a moment before.

He sighed and rolled his eyes at me. "I'm working for her former fiancé, Martin Zarkov. He wants to know where she's going, who she's with, and all that kind of stuff. I was looking for her will in her apartment. I can't believe she didn't tell you he'd be looking for that," Dave said, enjoying knowing more than I did.

"Why would he want to see her will?" I asked, with dawning comprehension.

"If you had a brain you could figure it out for yourself."

He was right. I had been an idiot.

Well, maybe not an idiot, but certainly no more than the second smartest unknown detective in Chicago.

"He wants to know if he's still in it," I said, proving I had a brain after all, albeit one that needed kickstarting every so often.

"Brilliant. I stand corrected."

"Did you find the will?"

"Of course."

"Is he still in it?"

"Yes," Dave said. I noticed he was trying to keep one eye on the street.

"Do you think he plans to kill her for it?"

Dave hesitated before answering, his caution restraining him. "Of course."

"The bloodsucking scum," I said.

"Ha!" Dave's laugh was staged. "That's rich, from you."

Why hadn't she told me about it? What did she have to hide? Wouldn't she want protection? What was her game?

I would have to go for her jugular and ask her some more penetrating questions. "Do you plan to stop him getting away with it?"

"Of course."

"Good. Thanks, Dave. You can go now."

"Oh, one more thing."

Dave swung at me, but I parried before he knew I had moved. I always could beat Dave in a fight. My years in Army intelligence stood me well. Thanks Uncle Sam.

"Very good," Dave complimented me, looking me straight in the eye, immune to my hypnotic gaze. Then his heel came down on my foot.

"Ow!"

"That's for nearly dropping a safe on me."

I should have seen that coming. "Touché. I hope I never see you again," I said, meaning every word. Dave made his way back to the street to find Jessica again and continue his surveillance, doing his best to keep to the shadows and stay out of the line of sight of... something. He got to the end of the alley when I quit watching him for only a second, distracted by some gum on my shoe.

I heard the vague muffled report of a rifle. Silenced. I couldn't tell what direction it came from, but I looked at Dave and saw him crumple to the ground. I ran to where Dave lay on the sidewalk. My lifelong friend, my best competition, the only one who knew my secret, was dead.

I regretted what I had just said to Dave. He wasn't such a bad egg. I'd only seen him rarely and sporadically for the last decade, but I would avenge him.

Evening fell as the last slivers of sunlight disappeared. A creature of the night, I was in my element, ready for action.

My first suspect could only be Martin Zarkov. Ideas and scenarios were already forming in my mind about the far-reaching plans and ambitious manoeuvres of this mysterious man. I just hoped he didn't know who, or what, I was. I could only keep Jessica safe if I could keep myself safe.

I examined the scene, working quickly because the shooter would be on the move now. There was a bullet mark on the ground, giving me an angle and direction. The shot had come from above and across the street.

There was a tall building with lots of windows. The bullet must have come from there. I wanted to cross over to cover the exits.

But I was too late. Even as I made my way across the busy street, a man dressed in a long black coat, hat, and sunglasses, was just leaving the building via the fire escape. He acted no more suspiciously than if he had been going to church on a Sunday morning, except for the silenced sniper's rifle he carried.

I no longer needed my sunglasses now it was dark, and took them off to get a good look at him.

I had never laid eyes on Martin Zarkov before, but I had no doubt that this was him.

I couldn't get to Zarkov before he got into a waiting car—actually more of a goods van in as-new condition, as though it had been garaged as soon as it came off the assembly line—and drove away. Lucky for me my ride was parked in the same parking lot that he had just left.

Keeping my headlights off, I got behind the wheel and sped off in pursuit of my quarry.

Overtaking ten or twenty other cars, I got Zarkov's vehicle back in sight. I followed him, keeping a few other vehicles between us. I didn't go very far before we both had to stop at a red light on a busy intersection.

My keen eyes saw Jessica blending into the crowd of people in the street making use of the crosswalk.

There were also a lot of cops mixed into the crossing multitude. I didn't know what they were doing there, but I wished they would go away.

Zarkov noticed Jessica too. His van, despite the red light, peeled out in a wide arc. I stamped my foot down on the accelerator the moment I noticed Zarkov's car moving. His path would take him to where Jessica was crossing the wide intersection.

Murder, cold-blooded, calculated, with no pretence of "making it look like an accident". I had perhaps two seconds. I gunned the engine and turned hard, nudging the car in front of me but enabling me to cut the corner and intercept Zarkov before he reached the pedestrian crosswalk. Jessica, hemmed in by the slow-moving crowd, was a sitting duck, as were the cops and other pedestrians.

I collided with Jessica's would-be vehicular assassin, sending both of our cars safely away from her in a crunching sprawl. Both our vehicles came to rest with their noses smashed straight through a wall, probably a big surprise to the diners in the cafe scant feet away from our headlights. Bricks and rubble dropped and thudded onto the car hoods, to the cafe patrons' consternation. So much for Zarkov's as-new van—the wall had not been kind to it, and it was barely more than a mass of metal now.

And so much for following at a safe distance.

The cops and others whose lives we had risked in our manoeuvres were unhurt, as was my quarry. An unflustered Zarkov got out of his van and ran in Jessica's direction, his body language screaming bloody murder.

I tried to open my door but it was jammed by the warping of the car's frame. In my frantic effort to get out, I wrenched the door handle clean off. Wasting precious seconds, I braced myself and kicked the door out, propelling it twenty feet away.

I was on the move again. I could see Zarkov grab Jessica and run across the street with her. She struggled against him, bless her, but for a lean man he was powerful, carrying her away with the least possible effort.

I pursued him with my gun drawn, heedless of the reactions of the throng of pedestrians, who until now had not reacted to our shenanigans. Now they parted like the Red Sea. Despite the apparent ease with which he kept Jessica moving, an unencumbered man like me was always going to be faster than he was. I gained ground until I thought I was close enough for him to hear me.

"Stop!" I shouted.

Zarkov turned himself and wrenched Jessica around to face me, keeping her in front of him as a human shield. I recognised the tracheal choke hold he immobilised her with—I had learned it myself in the army, and had used it against a few Krauts. He continued backing away briskly toward the building that he had first come out of, or one almost exactly like it. "No, you stop. Drop your gun or the girl dies." Zarkov smiled. "You see? I do not need a gun to beat you, Mr Stone."

I considered my options for a moment, and they weren't good. I was a good shot, but in the moment I would need to take aim at Zarkov's gloating head he could effortlessly crush Jessica's trachea with a simple pressure from his forearm, killing her instantly. My options were not good.

I tossed my gun toward him and it clattered to the ground near his feet.

As I had hoped he would, Zarkov stooped to pick the gun up, not easy while maintaining a chokehold on a woman. He took his eyes off me and relaxed his grip on her. Jessica, the feisty little minx, took the opportunity to try to push him over.

I dashed toward Zarkov, getting quite close, but he regained his hold on Jessica. Her wheezing breath was loud and clear as he gripped her neck that little bit too tightly.

I stopped.

Zarkov tried again to pick up the gun, again executing the difficult manoeuvre of bending down while maintaining a hold on his hostage, and this time he met no resistance from his now compliant victim.

But when he pointed my gun at me and started shooting, I resisted. I dove for cover behind a concrete planter, but I had been hit in the chest. It hurt, but there wasn't much bleeding—my low haemoglobin again—I'd have to get some more from somewhere.

The firing stopped, and I looked out from behind my cover.

Zarkov continued retreating to the building, keeping my gun pointed in my direction while he disappeared inside via the front door. Jessica was handled along, looking unperturbed—either she was confident I'd rescue her, or she had some trick up her sleeve. I left my hiding place and followed them in, cautiously so I wouldn't get shot again.

He moved pretty fast, and before I got to the stairs he was already up and out of my view.

I gave chase, but stopped halfway to the first floor. There had to be a better way than just following him. I was playing his game. That was no good. I had to make him play mine. There was a window here leading out onto the fire escape. I climbed through.

I discarded my two-tone oxfords and took the iron stairs, climbing two floors.

Zarkov and Jessica were visible through a grimy window—did nobody ever clean this place?—just before they went out of sight down a hallway and up more stairs. I ascended another flight of metal stairs, not making a sound.

Bingo!

Zarkov was backing toward me, nearing the window.

"Come on detective!" Zarkov shouted. Were his nerves beginning to show, to fray around the edges? "Try something. I dare you! But remember, I've got her neck in my hand!"

I was close to the window now, and so was Zarkov, only a foot away from me on the other side of the dirty glass.

I reached straight through the glass, shredding the skin of my hands as it shattered. I grabbed Zarkov's collar and dragged him backward through the window. Taking my pistol out of his hand, I embraced him in an iron grip. "And now, I've got your neck."

I bared my teeth and let him get a good look at my fangs before I sunk them into the flesh of his neck. His blood was rich and warm, and I drank, draining him as his body went flaccid.

Replete, I threw his lifeless body over the railings and watched him fall.

My hands were bleeding, but such was my satisfaction, and so shot through with fresh energy was I, that I scarcely noticed.

Despite her ordeal, Jessica played it cool as she climbed out to join me on the fire escape.

She removed some hankies from her pockets. "Those should heal nicely," she said, wrapping them around my mangled hands. "But now your secret is out."

"I guess so. I'll be hunted down. Unless I can persuade you to keep it quiet."

"I'll make you an offer," she said as her lips formed a grin, "I'll keep your secret if you'll keep mine." She smiled. Her own fangs gleamed pearly white.

Taking a moment to process this, I needed to know what had motivated her to set this chain of events into motion. "Why didn't you tell me what Zarkov was looking for?"

"Because then you would have taken me away for protection, and apprehended him alive," Jessica seethed, the hurt of love showing through in her detestation. "When he and I were together he treated me so badly... I wanted him dead, and I knew you could see to that."

I shook my head. "You could have done it yourself. You've got the teeth for it."

"No," she rebuked. "Like you, I have to live a life, even if I am undead. But no jury would convict you for saving my life."

"How many other dark secrets do you have, doll?"

"Enough to keep you interested."

"You know, you're almost a match for me."

"Almost?" Inclining her head downward slightly, she looked up at me, raising an eyebrow.

I drew closer to her, leaning, directing my mouth toward hers. She did the same, her lips red and slightly parted.

Did I really want to get involved with someone like this? She was hard, dark, secretive. And yet, I could feel her breath on me, and almost taste her perfume.

The satisfaction of a job well done and the anticipation of my reward kept me moving infinitesimally closer. Her lips were a fraction of an inch from mine, but there was no hurry.

We continued drifting closer together, reducing the tiny fraction of an inch to almost nothing, until finally...

A deafening ring, like the bells of Notre Dame, came between us. She was wrenched away from me at a thousand miles a second, as the seedy urban surroundings dissolved like wet paint under a fire hose.

Chapter 3 – Out

As always, your seventy decibel alarm clock brings you back when you would much rather have remained asleep. The clock has a crack across the top, which grows fractionally as you bring your fist down on the snooze button.

Not really wanting to get up you nevertheless sit upright and open your eyes as wide as you can until they tear up and relieve the sleepy sting the night has left you with. You rub the moisture into your eyes and stare absently into space, remembering the life you lived in your sleep.

You want the dream to come back, to get the chance to finish it, to kiss the girl and live happily ever after. But it's too late. It won't happen while you're awake.

The movie posters adorning your walls, lovingly and expensively framed, look down on you with their iconic characters. The undersea world of the Nautilus and the brooding Captain Nemo, possibly actor James Mason's finest hour, in Disney's "20,000 Leagues Under the Sea" dominates the wall opposite your bed. To your left a framed Bogart the gumshoe and Bacall the femme-fatale look sultrily into each other's eyes while pondering the confusing events of "The Big Sleep". To the right, Clint Eastwood as The Man With No Name, whose head floats over the Italian title of "A Fistful of Dollars" in the breakaway role for the then little known thirty-five year old actor. Over your bed a glinting sword dominates a painted battle—horses and armour, fire and ice, swords and spears—depicting John Boorman's "Excalibur". On the floor, propped against a wall, rests a framed Bela Lugosi, his hand at Helen Chandler's neck, as the quintessential vampire "Dracula".

Movies used to be your passion, a hobby and fascination you shared with—

You've kept the posters up for the last two years, but their frames need dusting.

You get out of bed, semi-prepared to face the day's music, which will likely be cloying and discordant.

You drive your car—not the armed response vehicle with all the windows shot out, but your own personal car—into the car park of your inner city police station. There's a lot of crime in the city—the pimps, drug dealers, and armed robbers never seem to know when to stop—and your police station is big.

The car park however is not big. You find an inconvenient place to park, seemingly requiring a can opener to get out of the car.

Leaving the vehicle and entering the building's reception area which is already filling up with the morning's thugs, you pause for a deep breath. King Arthur's agenda will, no doubt, fail to match with yours.

Under the influence of fluorescent lights and the incessantly complaining public, you are buzzed in and through the door with the "no entry to the public" sign. You sigh with relief, out of the realm of "the public".

You are now in privileged space, the hallowed halls, within the brotherhood of the police, where what happens in the station stays in the station—except for all the leaks to The Oracle.

Your colleagues speak their good morning greetings to you, but you keep walking and respond not at all.

Though you don't look any of them directly in the eye, you can see in your peripheral vision what their faces give away: you're not endearing yourself to them.

You see Dave without looking directly at him. It's been quite a while, but in years gone by you went out for beers with him, and occasionally even joked and laughed with him and his constant string of girlfriends. Bert, who replaced you as Dave's friend, is with him as well, grinning his dopey grin. He's of below average intelligence, but a good cop just the same.

You continue past them.

"Good morning to you, too," Bert mutters, probably thinking you can't hear him.

Maybe a response is justified. You stop, still looking straight ahead.

"Why say what's already been said? If I said good morning to you once, however long ago, why does it need to be reiterated daily? It's simply a waste of time. Think of all the hours which could be reclaimed if nobody bothered with 'good morning'."

You resume walking. Without having to look at him, you can guess at the look on Bert's face.

"Give him a break," Dave says, showing his usual inexhaustible sympathy. "He had a very bad night last night."

"I've had bad nights before," Bert says, "but I don't never let it give me no bad attitude."

"That's a double—" Dave counts on his fingers. "—triple negative."

"What?" Bert is justifiably confused.

A uniformed constable appears directly in front of you. You attempt to get around him, but the guy is nimble and stays in front of you, blocking your path.

"Stone!" the constable says directly into your face.

You glance around the area before looking him in the eye. "Who, me?" you say.

"King Arthur wants to see you in his office, asap!" Having said what he came to say, the young uniform gets out of your way.

You check your grey suit, tie, and cuffs reflected in an internal window as you make your way through the labyrinth of corridors. You don't have to make a particularly good impression for King Arthur, but so what?

When you arrive at the Superintendent's office you knock on the door, but then you think better of it and fling it open.

The muscled bulk of Superintendent Philip Arthur is seated behind his desk. Not managing to get into the gym very much these days, he sports an increasingly bulky belly. He is reading a newspaper, a filthy sordid rag entitled "The Oracle" while fingering his well groomed ginger moustache.

For some reason, even though he sent for you, he isn't waiting for you and ready to talk. "You wanted to see me?" you say.

Arthur continues reading his newspaper for a bit, just to keep you waiting.

You consider turning around to leave, but that would be disrespectful.

"I know this is just your tactic for imposing your authority," you say, "because you don't really think I've got nothing better to do than stand in front of your desk and twiddle. So did you actually want something?"

The Superintendent puts his newspaper down on his desk like a preacher pounding his Bible against the pulpit, and glares at you.

"Yeah, two things." Reluctance exudes from Superintendent Arthur's pores. "While I'd like to smack you down for your insubordination, I am first obliged to mention a matter of urgent practical importance." He clears his throat. "Remember this guy Steven Gates—"

Arthur makes the effort to rise from his seat just long enough to hand you a picture of a man you vaguely recognise.

"—who you put away a couple years ago for attempted murder? Well, he's on the street again."

You shrug your shoulders. "So?"

He holds his hands in front of him and shakes his head. "I just thought you might like to know," the Superintendent says, "just in case he comes looking for you. If you're not interested, fine. I've done my duty." Arthur looks down at his newspaper, giving you a chance to examine the photograph.

"What am I going to do? Hire a bodyguard? You don't seem to be offering me the job of finding the guy and bringing him in."

You wait for a response, in vain, before handing the picture back. "And the second thing? I've got work to do."

Looking up again, the Superintendent holds the newspaper out to you. "Have you read the paper this morning?"

He continues holding the paper out. "I never do," you say, ignoring it.

"Clever man," Arthur says as he spreads the paper out on his desk. "I wouldn't want you to break that tradition, so I'll summarise. A front page article by Lawrence Murphy in today's paper tells our beloved public about last night's… incident."

"So?"

"Well, he wasn't entirely truthful."

"Incredible!" You do your best to look shocked. "You don't think he'll set some sort of precedent, do you?"

"This is more serious than you think." You've got him now. The veins on his neck and temples are turning red as he fights down his exasperation. "They've made it look as if it's all your fault that one of our people was killed. They're accusing you of extreme cowardice on the job. In the editorials they said…" Arthur presses his fat finger down on the newspaper. He puts his reading glasses on, focusing on the tiny newsprint. "I'll read it to you. 'And where was constable Stone hiding while all the shooting was going on? How was he the only one left uninjured?'"

"Now you know why I don't read the paper, watch the news, or talk to reporters."

"Didn't you hear what it said?" His face reddens, though not enough to match the redness of his veins. "Those words aren't the normal, ostensibly impartial and detached, words of newspaper copy. This reporter is going after you, big style, and the paper's letting him. They're calling for your resignation."

"They know what they can do with their suggestions," you say.

"The public are behind them." The redness of his face and veins, and bloodshot zones appearing in his eyes, tell you that King Arthur is behind them as well. "Important people all over town are ringing up supporting the paper's suggestion."

"No surprises there. Is this really important? The public have never liked cops. And the papers have never liked me."

"We want the public to like us. We need their support. We also need the support of the press."

"Well," you say, "that all sounds very well. Your predecessor was just as concerned about our PR. But there's not much we can do about it, is there?"

"Maybe there is. Out of all the men on the force, do you know who's most responsible for our problems with the press and the public?"

"I'm sure I haven't got the slightest idea."

"I'm sure you have. If you didn't always treat journalists like they were leeches—"

"They are."

"Not all of them, and we can't afford to be prejudiced that way." Arthur's protruding veins grew so red they were purple. "And most civilians see you in a pretty bad light, too, because the newspaper tells them about you, and they believe it—"

"That's not my fault," you interrupt.

"—and they assume it's true of all of us," he says, literally spitting out his words. "It is your fault that you give them anything to talk about in the first place."

Your picture stares at you from the newspaper splayed across the Superintendent's desk, an archive photo—The Oracle uses it often. You pick the tabloid up and punch the picture with your finger several times. "This is irresponsible reporting," you snarl. "It's nothing to do with me."

"Okay, yes, you've been misrepresented in this article, but that's only because they already hate you." He holds his palms up in front of him, entreating you to understand.

You do understand. "That's only because they're—"

"I know what they are, but you can't change that, and all you're doing is making bad PR for the rest of us."

"Yes, I know," you say. "We've been here before."

The Superintendent sniggers reluctantly. "You do take on board our equality and diversity policy, I'll give you that. You snub uniforms and plainclothes, inferior and superior, black and white, Christian and Muslim. Discrimination has no part in your creed. And that's your problem."

He turns serious again as the colour drains from his arteries, veins, eyes, and face. Arthur speaks. "I'm recommending you go on holiday until this thing dies down."

You try to speak, and fail. You look from the newspaper in your hand to Arthur and back again several times. "I— I— I can't do that! I need to work. I've got cases to finish."

"What is the matter with you?" Do you see a look of sympathy on his pale face? "Anybody else would love some time off."

"I'm not anybody else!" Your face is hot. It's your turn to go red.

"Look, Don, you're an alright cop, and I sympathise with your problems, but there's nothing special about you.

You've just suffered a little more, that's all."

"I didn't ask for your sympathy," you say, feeling the heat in your ears. "I only asked you for my job!"

"Inspector Stone!" The Superintendent shouts at you, his face suddenly red again, his veins purple. "I'm not going to tolerate any more of your insubordination! You're on suspension." He leans toward you, putting his hands on his desk to bear his weight. You see the crimson threads in the whites of his eyes. "That means no pay!"

Taking advantage of your speechlessness, the Superintendent leans in closer to you. He resumes his normal colour as he calms down, lowering his voice as if you and he weren't the only people in the room. "It's been almost two years, Don. It's time to pull yourself together."

The vein game is no fun any more. You exit the Superintendent's office. "Stone! My newspaper!" he shouts after you. You're not going back in there, so you ignore him. If he wants to arrest you for theft there are more than enough cops here to take you down.

There's nothing for you here now. You might as well go home. Of course, there's nothing much for you there either.

As you re-emerge into the corridor and take up a brisk walking pace, somehow, Dave appears at your side. "How did it go? Are you going to be okay?"

When you don't respond, Dave says, "How were his veins?"

You keep walking, disinclined to speak, but the question is irresistible. "Livid."

Dave smiles at that.

"So what happened?"

"I don't want to talk about it," you say.

"Oh, come on, we've worked together a long time. You can talk to me."

You stop, take a deep breath, and rub your eyelids with

your fingers. "I'm on a long holiday. Me and King Arthur had a disagreement."

"'King Arthur and I'."

You roll your eyes and resume walking.

The building's exit gives you an easy out. One abrupt turn, and you open and attempt to slam the door behind you.

No matter how much force you apply, the hydraulic door closer prevents the door from slamming. The door fails to make a loud, unexpected noise, and nobody looks at it, startled.

You leave the building, still carrying the Superintendent's copy of The Oracle.

The expansive car park shaded by expansive trees gives the cemetery a feeling of open space unknown in most parts of the city.

The sun glints off your sunglasses as you get out of your car in your immaculate suit. If you weren't carrying a bundle of brightly coloured flowers you could be mistaken for a royal bodyguard. The cemetery is crisscrossed with paths and dotted with benches, but you could navigate it blind. You pass hundreds of gravestones of varying sizes before you find the one you're looking for.

This bench is yours. You paid for it and the engraved plaque that adorns it. It was worth the money too. It has seen a lot of use in your idle hours. You sit down and find yourself staring at a marble headstone. It's basic, no frills, inscribed, "Melissa Marie Stone, beloved wife". You could have added a lot more, but you wouldn't have known where to start. Or where to finish. It shows some dates too, but you avoid looking at those.

In this place you are free to sit down and be quiet. You can be alone with your thoughts. It's your bench. It's her bench.

Sitting here is relaxing, in a way.

You're free to remember her life. Which you refuse to do. Free to remember the things she said, which you refuse to do. Free to indulge in grief, free to weep, which you refuse to do.

As you stare at the headstone, soaking up the melancholy atmosphere, you sense a man approaching, though he makes no sound.

"Afternoon, Mr Stone," the groundskeeper says, holding his flat cap in both hands in front of him. "I'm glad to see you brought her some new flowers."

You look up at the fluffy clouds, taking in the shapes. That one looks like a rabbit.

The gardener continues. "She was a wonderful young lady."

The headstone is very white. It hasn't worn much in two years. You admire it at some length.

"Well, if there's anything I can do for you…"

You think back, involuntarily remembering Melissa's smile, and her frown.

"You can stop disturbing me," you say to the old goat.

At the edge of your vision you see him looking as if he wants to say something, starting and stopping, taken aback as if he shouldn't have come to expect this kind of reaction by now. That's the problem with having a short old person's memory.

"Why do people want to interfere with what isn't their business?" you say. "Don't you get sick of well-meaning people who talk and yammer when what they should do is shut up? Two years of enduring them now. It seems an eternity."

"Mr Stone, a little politeness wouldn't cost you anything."

"How do you know what it won't cost me?"

The gardener apparently thinks better of saying anything more, and leaves you alone. At last.

Now that he's gone, the tear you've been holding back escapes and runs down your cheek.

You wipe it away.

"Man up, Stone," you say almost inaudibly.

You don't know how much longer you stay soaking it up. Silence, solitude, sorrow—that's what you came for. The cemetery is perfect for that kind of reflection. Until the old goat—Jim, or Geoff, or Gene, whatever his name is—gets in on the act. Yes, Melissa always had time for him, living as he did a few doors down from yours. She used to tell you off about your lack of patience with him.

Well, now you can tell yourself off.

But you've got places to go, people to see, havoc to wreak.

All that's left to do here is to lay your flowers lovingly across the grave. The groundskeeper would prefer you put them upright in a vase. Oh well. He'll have to suck it up.

The words "The Oracle" are written in big bold three-dimensional backlit professionally sculpted letters—albeit in a conservative typeface. The lettering adorns the wall behind the reception desk, where the receptionist sits, looking at a magazine while she files her nails.

"May I help you?" the receptionist asks. Go easy on her—she doesn't know you. Walking on past, you ignore the girl, her magazine, and her nails.

Why would you need help? You know where the newsroom is. You conducted a successful drugs raid in this very building only a few years ago.

The receptionist stands, dropping her nail file on the desk. "Excuse me sir, are you here to see someone?"

"Yes," you say without stopping.

Pushing through the big doors into the circulatory system of the building, you orient yourself toward its limply beating heart while you hear the receptionist behind you say, "Security," into a telephone.

You have all the time in the world. You don't hurry. You walk an inconspicuous pace, tightening your tie, checking your buttons and cuffs as you go.

Perhaps their security people are busy preventing electronic viruses and limiting staff Internet access.

You've been walking for a couple of minutes now and no one has even attempted to stop you. The corridor is busy. Execs wearing suits much more expensive than yours, reporters with loosened ties and rolled up sleeves, secretaries, tea ladies, gophers, all wearing security badges hanging from their necks or clipped to their belts—and no one has given you a second look, despite your lack of badge.

You get into a lift with a lot of suits who, like you, are neat and tidy. Unlike you, they are wearing security badges.

But this is a lift, where people look only at their familiar acquaintances, and the rest look at the ceiling. Except you—your'e a cop, and you look at their faces.

The elevator opens.

A few seconds more and you're in the newsroom making straight for Lawrence Murphy's desk. You find him seated, typing away at his keyboard.

You stand in front of him, daring him to notice you, but he keeps typing until he reaches for his phone. "Mr Murphy," you say, lacking patience.

Meeting your eyes at last, Murphy notices you and, surprised but not dismayed, looks venomous daggers at you as he leans back in his chair and comfortably folds his hands across his stomach. One of the Oracle's senior reporters, Murphy can get away without wearing a tie. He sports a short sleeve shirt, revealing the nicotine patch on his arm. His smile reveals his browning teeth.

"Well, well, if it isn't PC Stone," he says, bringing one hand up to finger the cigarette behind his ear, wishing he could light up. "On your day off today, constable?"

"Inspector," you say. "Constable is for rookies."

"Oooh. Inspector. Proud of your achievements, are you?"

"Why not? They're more than yours," you say.

Two security guards seem to have only just caught up with you.

"Mr Murphy," one of the security guards says, "this bloke's trespassin'. 'E giving y'any trouble?"

"It's okay," Murphy says. "He's with me."

"Fine," the security guy says. They're reluctant to leave, wanting to assert their authority, of which they actually have very little, and rarely get to show it. "Let us know if you change your mind." The guards leave.

"What's on your mind, Inspector?" Murphy continues playing with the cigarette on his ear, crumpling it and causing flecks of tobacco to fall on the floor.

"That article you wrote about me was in extremely bad taste, and you're going to print a retraction." It's more of a question than a statement, since you're sort of hoping he'll refuse.

"I just write 'em as I see 'em, so to speak."

"You got to see them to write them."

"Yeah. Well, my sources are very reliable—"

"Sources?" you interrupt. "What sources? You're getting information from cops on the ground?"

"—and I did see the results of your," Murphy continues, pausing to emphasise the next word, "wonderful performance."

"You're going to look very funny with no teeth," you say before taking a deep breath, trying to fight down the growing exasperation.

Murphy stands, his face a picture of incredulity. "You'd rough me up? Here?"

You bite your words out through clenched teeth. "Are you going to get that retraction printed?"

"I wouldn't if you paid me. You're a menace to the people of this city, and I'm going to make sure everybody knows it."

"You're uncooperative," you say.

"As a politician," he adds.

A necktie would have been a good handle but Murphy isn't wearing one, so you grab him by his collar and drag him onto his desk. He scarcely attempts to resist, and nor do you, as your fist connects hard with his jaw once, then twice. You still have him by the scruff of his neck with your other hand, damp from the sweaty collar of his cheap shirt, so you lift him up slightly and thump his head down onto the surface of the desk with a rich resonant echo.

You raise your balled fist high for another strike at his begging jaw when flashes of light compete for your attention. Distracted from your task, satisfying though it is, you look around you. Almost everyone in the newsroom has cameras trained on you, clicking, beeping, flashing.

Realising you're striking a tantalising pose, fist held high above your helpless victim, it's time to stand down. You've done enough damage here, in more ways than one.

You let go of Murphy, letting him slide off the desk and onto the floor with a thud.

The crowd of photographers back off as a unit, giving you plenty of room to pass as you exit the newsroom. You're allowed to pass through the corridors unmolested by security or anyone else.

Finding yourself back at the reception desk, you look at the extruded text on the wall behind the receptionist: The Oracle.

"You know," you say to her, "those words lie."

The poor girl just looks at you like a rabbit looks at oncoming headlights.

Your hands are giving you trouble. One hurts, and both are shaking. Weak-kneed and high on adrenaline, you need to sit down and let it pass. But not here. It's necessary to get out of the building first. Security may yet catch up with you.

Night fell. The day has gone quickly.

Standing before one of the massive windows looking out onto the runway, you observe the night sky. In the panorama before you the plane comes in from the left, its landing lights illuminating the rainy night. Like a lazy bird, it touches down on the runway surrounded by hazy spray as it continues, slowing down until it eventually goes out of sight at the extreme right of your view.

Turning your attention from the outside to the inside, it only takes a minute to find an arrivals display. You find the listing you're looking for and check it for the third time in an hour. It's on time—it landed forty long minutes ago.

Even though there is a clock clearly visible on the arrivals board, you look at the chunky Lorus watch on your wrist. It's quite big, and sometimes gets caught on things, but where watches are concerned you have always felt that bigger is better.

It won't be long now. You smile subtly.

Turning around, you return to the arrivals area and notice the crowd of people, some holding placards telling who they're looking for or what hotel they're from. You go and stand among them, blending in with the limousine drivers, the family members, and those waiting for loved ones.

Passengers begin to trickle out of the customs area carrying, pushing, or dragging their luggage. One by one, the greeters find the greetees, welcoming them with hand-shakes, hugs, kisses, and kind words, some of them enjoying the euphoria of long delayed reunions. You take in each one without recognition, which is a good thing because if you recognised them they would probably be criminals.

The plane has arrived safely. The airport isn't under a security lock-down. Has Customs stopped her for something? Is Airport Security having a word with her? Did she miss her flight? Unlikely.

And then she emerges. For a second your guts feel empty, your heart stops, and you forget to breathe. And that also is a good thing.

As she makes her way past the security railings and all the other arriving passengers, you take in her appearance. Unlike the femme fatale from your dream, this Jessica, the real Jessica, dresses comfortably and wears glasses, looking like the schoolteacher she is. Neither made up nor bejewelled, she has the prettiest face and figure you know, unadorned and unglamorous. She pushes before her a trolley overburdened with luggage.

The barrier that separates you from her is only a woven seat-belt-thing stretched between some poles, practically daring you to duck under, but you wait as Jessica makes her way around it. It seems an eternity, but it's really only a few seconds, before she's hugging you tightly.

The grip of her arms around you, the soft brush of her hair against your neck, the wrap of your arms around her, give you a kind of satisfaction.

You hold her for as long as you dare—as long as you can get away with.

"Donovan, it's so good to see you!" she says with a smile on her lips and warmth in her voice. "How are you doing?"

"Oh, never mind that," you say. "How are you? I've missed you."

"Good," she says. "I'm glad to know somebody misses me. I've missed you too."

Jessica starts to push the trolley along, attempting to hide the difficulty she finds in getting it moving.

"I can't imagine why," you say.

"Me neither," Jessica says. "Oh well."

"You always say such nice things," you sneer.

"Well, you know, that's just me."

"Let me take care of that for you," you say as you take the unwieldy trolley.

"Can I trust you with it?" Jessica says.

"Of course not."

You jauntily begin to push the trolley, but you're surprised when it hardly wants to move. "You must have friends in high places—"

"Well I did sit sit next to a nice old lady on the plane," she says, a twinkle in her eye.

"—because I don't think they normally would let a passenger carry four bags full of bricks," you say, making a show of stressing and straining with the weight of the luggage-laden trolley. "And I'm pretty sure all the airlines have a limit of two bags."

"Yeah, I know. I had to pay extra for the excess bags. Now be nice. I've been gone a long time."

"And it's wonderful to have you back, but not all your dead weight." You feel you're just about getting control of the trolley.

"Yeah, well one of my dead weights got split by the baggage handlers." Sure enough, there was a tear in one of her bags temporarily covered over with duct tape. "I've got to go over to the airline's help desk to get a claim form or something. You stay here with these."

"Yes madam," I said, giving a mock salute. "I'll guard them with my worthless life."

"You do that," Jessica says as she walks away. You watch her, knowing it's not polite to stare, but unable to take your eyes off her. Of course if she looked at you you would look away and pretend to be examining the wall.

"Sir, here is a free gift for you." A scruffily dressed young man with a shaved head is standing at your side offering you a plastic flower with a printed label attached.

"Thank you, yes," you say as you accept the gift.

"Would you care to make a donation?" This collector wears no badge and has no official donation box, simply holding his hand out.

This guy might just need some bus fare to get home—who knows? You reach into your pocket and, without looking at it, remove a handful of jingling things which you drop in his hands.

"I think you'll need these," the collector says, handing you back your car keys while keeping the coins—bus fare indeed! "Thank you for your contribution. Would you like me to chant a blessing for you?"

You look him in the eye. "I think not."

"Have a good evening anyway," he says as he turns to go.

"A tip," you say. The collector stops to listen to you. "You're not actually allowed to do this here. Watch out for the security guards and cameras."

The young man beams at you with a grateful smile. "Thank you. Have a good evening sir."

"I'll try," you say to his back as he leaves.

"They say they'll reimburse me," Jessica says, having reappeared unnoticed at your other side. "Who was that man?"

"Just some bum," you say.

"What did he want?" Jessica says, watching him go.

"Money."

"Did you give him some?"

"Of course," you say. "Do you think I'm heartless?"

"Of course not Donovan," Jessica says. "You're all heart. That's why you're my best friend," she says as she wraps her arms around one of yours.

She gives your arm a quick squeeze and releases it.

You clear your throat. "So we can leave now?"

"Yes."

In a few minutes, back at your car, you have hoisted two of the heavy bags into the boot, which is now full. You close it.

You open the rear passenger door and pick up the third bag. As you strain to lift it into the car Jessica says, "Now be careful with that." You grunt and groan exagerratedly and shoot her a mocking dirty look.

You set it down against the protests of the springs and look at the fourth one with dread.

"Come on, just one more. Don't be a wimp," Jessica says, drumming her fingernails on the car, like a detached taskmaster.

"Let's just leave it," you protest. "You'll probably never notice the difference."

She narrows her eyes at you. "I told you to be nice."

At this hour the roads aren't busy, and you're making good time, enjoying Jessica's company.

"What were those men doing there?"

"I don't know," you say. "Hiding, or preparing an ambush. That's about all I can say."

"Come on, you must know more than that," Jessica said. "What were they doing in the Outlands? And why were you there?"

You frown and sigh. "It was a simple rundown. They'd been pursued there, and then lost. I was called in for support and try to find them. So were all the other units."

"And where were these guys they pursued from?"

"I was told it was a bank robbery in the city centre… but something about that doesn't add up. They then hightailed it to the Outlands and waited for us. Who can know what they were thinking? They were psychos."

There's a moment of silence as you run out of information to give her.

"Is that all?"

"Yes. I wasn't told very much, and I'm not on the case, so I'm not in the loop."

Jessica looks at you with something resembling disbelief. "If someone had just killed one of my friends and injured a lot of others, I'd want to know all about it."

"Well…" you stammer. "I don't know." The reflectors on the road surface glow orangely.

"What do you mean about something not adding up?"

"I don't know. A gut feeling I guess. I'm probably wrong."

"But what if you're not wrong? Don't you think you should follow your instincts?"

"Like I said, I'm not on the case. I'm not on any case," you say. You would put your head in your hands if you didn't need them on the steering wheel. "What does all that matter now, anyway? Three injured and one dead—that was the final score, and just because I couldn't shoot straight," you say.

She searches for the right thing to say. "Well, you were nervous." Jessica tries to be sympathetic. "Besides, I think you're sacrificing accuracy for dramatic effect."

"Damn right I was nervous," you say, expecting her to tell you off for swearing, "but I was the one in the best position to do something. If I could have kept a cool head…"

"Well, I couldn't have done any better if it had been me." We listen to the road noise for a few seconds. "Try to be realistic about it."

"Realistic?" You imagine fresh images of the previous night, almost interfering with your driving. "I can hardly even believe it really happened. It seems like a dream. Especially since I wasn't even hurt! The only proof it was real is that it was in the newspaper, and that's pretty shaky proof. No, that's not true. The proof is that my friends—I mean my colleagues—are in hospital. Or the morgue."

"I'm sorry." Jessica plays with the dials on the silent radio. "I wish there was something I could do."

All of a sudden you feel hot. You turn the heat down as the sweat beads on your forehead. The cooler air blowing against your damp brow chills you.

"So do I," you say, wiping your forehead with the back of your hand. "Anyway, as if that weren't enough, the press are trying to blame me for it."

"How can they do that?" she says, gesturing pleadingly, as if there was someone to entreat. "It wasn't your fault."

"Read The Oracle," you sneer. "Today's edition is on the back seat—if you can get it out from under that half-ton paperweight—I mean, your suitcase. You'll see how they can do it. That ass Lawrence Murphy wrote daggers at me. Even got me suspended from the force."

"Oh?" Jessica says. "Do you know him?"

"Er… not… not well."

Jessica shifts in her seat, taking a moment to watch the street lights and passing cars. You endure the relative silence of the engine's hum, and the bumps in the road, for a minute.

"Well, maybe we can talk about something a little more cheerful," Jessica says with a promising smile. "Are you seeing anybody these days?"

You pause, as if considering the question. "That's more cheerful? No, I'm afraid not."

"Nobody?"

"That's right."

"Why not?"

"No-one's asking."

"You're supposed to do the asking," she says in her best schoolteacher-to-pupil tone.

"Oh, so that's my problem. I'm so glad to have that solved."

You bring your car to a stop outside Jessica's grandmother's house, where Jessica makes her home whenever she's in town. Quite elderly now, Grandma has never failed to give Jessica a good home since her parents divorced unamicably when she was a child. Neither parent was able to look after her, so Jessica views Grandma as her surrogate parent.

You get out of the car and walk around to the passenger side to open Jessica's door for her while she waits for you to do so.

She gets out of the car and you close her door.

"I'm so glad chivalry is not dead." She opens the boot and hauls one of her cases out.

"Put that down," you say. "I've got this."

"I'll manage," Jessica says, struggling manfully. "I'm not as weak as I look."

Both of you drag her luggage out of the car with considerable difficulty.

Jessica is clearly struggling against the weight of the cases more than you are, but the two of you make it to the front door without collapsing. Repeating the process, you bring the other two bags as well.

You take the luggage into the dark and quiet house, and come out again.

Jessica gives you a big hug as she says, "Thanks for picking me up. I hate making you do that. I hate airports."

You return the friendly embrace and let her go. "A lot of people hate airports," you say. "I don't. I've done a lot of good work in airports."

"Well, tonight was no exception. So well done."

You clear your throat. "Of course, the airport isn't usually where I go to pick up women, but in your case I'm willing to make an exception."

"Oh yeah?" she says. "Where do you usually go?"

"Oh, you know… all the wrong places."

"Hmm. Well thank you anyway. You're a wonderful friend."

"Well… you're not so bad yourself," you say.

"Good night," she says, inching back into the house.

You loiter, fingering a wind chime hanging over the awning. She begins to shut the door.

"I'm sorry Donovan. I'd like to invite you in for a coffee, but I'm just so tired," she says. "Do you mind?"

"It's okay. One lives in hope. Good night."

Jessica waves as she gently closes the door, smiling a sympathetic apology.

It's not that late, but you've nothing else to do so you go home. Driving a round-about route because you're in no hurry, it's easier to mull things over from behind the wheel.

Your comfortable armchair in your over-tidy living room is overlooked by a lamp that creates a pool of light while leaving the rest of the room in darkness. To your side is an end-table on which is perched a steaming Irish coffee—minus the Irish.

The stolen copy of The Oracle, a publication you haven't read in detail for many years, has a lot of words about last night's events—and much to say about you—but nothing you didn't already know. Lawrence Murphy hasn't done a very good job at investigating.

But you didn't know about the letters the perps had sent to the press, detailing their sympathies with the causes of the oppressed peoples of Palestine, African-Americans, Al-

Qaeda, and the poor farmers of India—a long and unlikely list for a bunch of psychos.

And they threaten further "demonstrations". What kind of demonstrations?

You close the paper, folding it neatly, before you rub your eyes with your palms. The tiredness stings.

Chapter 4 – Swordplay

The virgin English countryside was undefiled by the work of man, except the well worn bridleway. The rolling hills, the green grass, the clouds threatening to pour rain upon us, the mud our horses laboured through, all combined to wish us a happy homecoming after our time spent on the continent.

The French, of course, had not been friendly to us, and Spain had been little better with its Moorish population raising swords against any who come from "Christian" nations, whatever their intentions.

My horse, laden with supplies and clanking armour, cantered jauntily obeying my familiar touch. This animal had become one of my most trusted friends, despite having been stolen from his Moorish master near the Straits of Gibraltar. I think the moor must have been cruel to him, because the beast took to me from the moment I killed his former rider. My sword had tasted more blood on this quest than was expected with someone of my station, but my master always encouraged me to hone my martial skills.

Sir Hudson rode next to me, regal, dignified, every inch the shining knight. Unlike my mount, his horse was free of encumbrances. Sir Hudson's saddle carried nothing except a sword in its scabbard and a crossbow, attached by leather thongs. Carrying his stuff was my work, a burden I gladly bore.

"At that time, I was but a squire, as thyself," Sir Hudson said, telling me the story for perhaps the tenth time. "But the king beheld me perform what he took to be an act of bravery. Verily, it was nothing any other would not have done in my stead, but the king was generous, and put me through the trials." He spoke of his triumph shamefacedly, reluctant to accept the praise for his own good work, preferring to exalt his king while abasing himself.

Sir Hudson's armour shone as brightly as I could keep it polished while we were between way stations, and the sun, momentarily shining from between the clouds, glinted into my eyes as it reflected from the polished surface. That shine was my handiwork, and I did it as unto the Lord.

I listened, visualising every word as he spoke. "They were arduous trials, but I persevered, and conquered, and the king knighted me. But have I not told thee the tale before?"

"Yes master, thou hast," I said earnestly. "I desire to hear it again because I, too, would one day be a knight of the round table. Alas, I lack the bravery and skill with the sword." I toyed with my horse's mane. Such ambition was not meet for me. My master had raised me up, as from the offscouring of all things, to far above my proper station already. Far be it from me noble knighthood.

I began my seventeenth year that summer. A precocious student, I had advanced more quickly than the other boys, and might have been able to accompany my master on his quests abroad at the tender age of fifteen. But Sir Hudson, my master, wisely advised me against the snare of pride, which he assured me was the worst of all sins, and he held me back, forcing me to maintain my training at the same pace as my peers. Nevertheless, his encouragements to me were lavish.

"Denigrate thyself not, young squire. Our quest is not yet done. What lieth ahead for thee, thou knowest not." He spurred his horse to a gallop, challenging me to relish the future and the unknown over the horizon. As was my duty, I followed, galloping after him while my horse strained only slightly under the greater burden it carried. After maintaining our speed long enough to cross the flat moors and approach the nearby hills, we slowed to allow our animals some breath, so not to spend them needlessly.

Sir Hudson could not have more sagely spoken had he been a seer, for as we rounded the next hillock our path was blocked by six assassins. Each was mounted, appearing as death on horseback, animals and riders clad in black armour, their attire appearing to take inspiration from the reputedly soundless and invincible slayers of the East. The black finish of their armour denied any reflection so that the dark knights appeared almost intangible. I prayed that we might shortly be given to test their tangibility with our blades.

To one side of the dark knights two winsome wenches—women of such appearance that a young man such as I might willingly chance his life—were seated on a single horse, their hands bound tightly to the bridle, chafing their delicate wrists.

"Sir Hudson." One of the dark knights spoke—I know not which—the hoarse growl of his voice exuding malice and evil. "Thy life is in peril. Except thou relinquish to us now the Holy Grail thou shalt perish in torment." They paused, waiting for my master's answer with patience bred from living while their opponents died.

As vigilant ebony statues, the dark knights rested their hands on the hafts of their scabbarded swords.

"In truth, I return from my quest to seek the Grail, and had I obtained it I would contend even to death to keep it. But know ye that I have not yet found it. Waste not your lives in combat for that which I possess not." My master's assured words emboldened me as well.

"It is noised abroad that thou hast the grail, and we will confirm this rumour. Dismount and submit." The dark knight's words echoed the same confidence with which Sir Hudson spoke. And yet, glancing at my master, I could descry no waver in his unmarked visage.

There was no question of my master's submission, and my duty was clear: if I did not follow my master, even to the death, I was unworthy of life. He kept his seat, so so must I.

The dark knights allowed us several seconds to consider our answer. At an apparently predetermined instant, when the seconds were expired the dark knights attacked, in perfect unison and with lightning speed.

Despite our distance from the dark knights, my master's sword was out and flashing in the same moment, ready to meet them ere they closed the gap. He had taught me well— I was no more than an instant behind him in my readiness. Sir Hudson and myself, expecting the black armour to be highly resistant, drew and hurled our heavy daggers with a power that sacrificed precision for force but nevertheless caught two of the knights squarely in their hearts. Crimson essence filled their wounded armour, and a little seeped out. With a crash they collapsed to the ground in motionless black and burgundy heaps.

The remaining four dark knights were instantly upon us two by two, attacking my master and myself in separate skirmishes with a ferocity matched by few other enemies of our quest, our king, our country, or our Lord.

From our commanding positions atop our horses bred for battle, we fought furiously, manoeuvring horses and swords in an effort to gain quarter on our foes, but we could do little more than maintain a defence.

I focused my senses on my own opponents, but nevertheless from one side I heard the metallic shriek of a sword piercing armour. Had he scored a kill? But no—my master himself gasped in pain. Never had I witnessed my master fail in battle, nor allow his armour to be scratched.

I slipped out from between my two attackers to assist my master. He had fallen off his horse, his shoulder rent and bleeding. One of his enemies slid off his horse and raised his sword.

In an instant I closed the distance between us. Spurring on my own mount to his best speed, I shouted a battle cry as I guided my animal to crash into the rider and send him sprawling, hopefully stunned. My master's chances were now better, with both his enemies dismounted, but danger loomed as his first attacker stood directly before him, poised to strike.

From atop my horse I struck downward to pierce the neck of my master's attacker, depriving the dark knight of his worthless and evil life before he could raise his sword.

I leapt down from my horse and attended to my fallen master. But a mere glance from Sir Hudson alerted me to the dark knight behind my back. As I turned to face him I saw that falling from his horse had done him no harm apart from dents and blemishes.

The now riderless horses milled about, oblivious to the melee except perhaps inasmuch as they preferred not to eat grass that had been sullied with blood.

Having caught me preoccupied with concern for my master, the dark knight disarmed me of my loosely held sword. My master would be displeased that I had lost my weapon, and my concern for his safety would be no excuse. Trusting that my opponent expected me to leap backward, I instead threw myself at him—thus preventing him arcing his sword against me. I wrestled savagely, as did he, but turning the element of surprise against him had given me the upper hand, which I pressed into his neck with deadly force. The knife blade built into the edge of my armoured hand released his lifeblood as it cut through his vein. At least this enemy would never again be taken unawares.

I turned to my master, bloodied but not beaten, who was now sitting up. He smiled, though his mien was pained.

"My thanks squire Donovan. Thou art truly a mighty man of valour," Sir Hudson said as he cast another warning glance. "Behind!"

I turned as my master gripped my hand to help himself up. We stood and faced our enemies, as our animals continued to forage blissfully, taking no interest in our squabbles where there was grass to be consumed.

The two remaining dark knights held the two wenches, their blades at the women's throats. I considered whether to throw myself on the enemy's mercy in exchange for the maidens' lives. Beauty such as theirs must be preserved whatever the cost.

"Cast aside your blades," a dark knight's throaty voice intoned with practiced but effortless threatening, "or these comely creatures hasten to their graves." The brutes inside the black armour could scarcely be men at all, else they could not threaten those lovely and innocent necks.

I waited, almost holding my breath with desperation to act. What would my master have us do? We could not knowingly be responsible for these women's deaths—unable as we were to disable the dark knights, for they were out of our reach—nor could we move against them ere they cut the women's throats.

Though unaware of and uninvolved in the situation unfolding around her, my master's horse, needing to replenish her energy after her long hard ride, had been tucking in greedily. Having probably espied some attractive grass on which to feed, the beast wandered in from the left to, in no particular hurry, interpose herself between the dark knights and ourselves.

Our view of the dark knights obscured, we drew our one remaining dagger each and raised them in readiness. How true my aim must be and how quickly I must let fly my blade if I were to save the damsel alive—and avoid killing her myself! That the dark knights were so much taller than the wenches meant they left their necks unobscured by captive female flesh, giving us one and only one target for our blades. No sooner had the horse moved far enough to the right, revealing again the dark knights and their captives, than we let fly our daggers. Now gone from my hand, I could only trust in the skills imparted to me by my master that my knife would find its proper mark.

Even flinching with the pain of his injury, my master's aim was truer. So close had my throw been to killing the maiden that she lost a lock of hair before my knife found its mark in the dark knight's neck. Her beauty sullied, I nevertheless consoled myself that her lock would grow again, and the fuller would white her raiment of the stain of her dead captor's blood. And no amount of staining or removal of hair could truly mar her loveliness—it was hers, and belonged not to her adornments.

As should befall any who would use maidens as surety— the stronger hiding behind the weaker—the two evil men fell dead to the ground with a mighty noise of armour. Confident I was that none would miss them, save possibly their own master, whoever that was.

Weeping tears of relief, the wenches ran to our feet and knelt before us, a fantasy of bliss I had never dared dream.

"I am thine, sir, body and soul, evermore," the lighter maiden said to Sir Hudson.

"And I thine, sir," said the darker to me. The fantasy escalated with each breath! The most beautiful creature in existence was mine, and I had done nothing I would not have done had she not been there.

"No, my lady," Sir Hudson said through teeth clenched with pain. "I am at thy service, for I am on a holy quest and have taken a vow. I release thee; seek thou a husband which spilleth no blood, and live in contentment." My noble master would gladly have been a martyr, had any been able to defeat him. But now he played the martyr for reasons of honour and integrity, and he would that I followed his example.

But the lady cast her eyes down. "Nay, for we are not virtuous women. True, we were the prisoners of the dark knights. But it was not always so. At the first we had other reasons for our bonds. We are unworthy of husbands or mercy. Only let me be thy servant, my lord. Put me to what use thou seest fit."

Such intimations of her crimes mattered little to me, so enamoured was I. Indeed, I merely desired her the more.

"And I am not worthy of thee, my lady," I said, hesitating, wondering if I should not abdicate my knightly aspirations for those of domesticity, "for I am but a lowly squire, and dare not but look upon thy heavenly beauty. Now, if thou hast lived a life of sin heretofore, then use well this gift of new life." Ah well. Self-denial has a certain beauty as well, so I have heard.

"Aye, go ye forth and sin no more, for you were dead and now live. Now ride to the village over yonder hill," my master said as he pointed the way. "The innkeeper will help you find your way home if you mention the name of Sir Hudson." He smiled gently at them—though his wounded shoulder made it difficult—putting them at their ease.

"Our thanks, kind sirs." They raised their heads, looking us in the eyes, embracing the boon we had granted them. "Only suffer us to gather herbs to soothe thy wound and dress it for thee." The damsel who spoke summoned up a smile. Her companion did the same. In that moment, their beauty increased tenfold, their faces truly shone forth the sun, otherwise hidden by clouds.

I held up a hand to stop her, now sensitive that my position at my master's side could be usurped. "Nay fair one, for that is my duty. My inculcation in my master's service comprehendeth the rudiments of the apothecary's art." I held up the medicine bag I kept on my belt.

"Then God be with you both," one of the women said while looking at me. I flatter myself I believe I saw in her a reluctance to bid us farewell, such was her desire to remain with me. But it was better that she seek a peaceful husband as my master had commanded them than to go with bloody and violent men such as we.

"And with you," Sir Hudson replied, manfully banishing the strain from his voice. Truly did my master need medicine.

My master took the wenches' hands and bade them rise. He reached out to them with his injured arm as they rose—I could almost feel his pain myself—giving no indication of discomfort and allowing our new friends to feel at ease and free of obligation.

"Your captors have no further use for their beasts," Sir Hudson said, making a sweeping gesture with his good arm to indicate the riderless horses of the dark knights. "Ride two and sell five. The animals' armour alone will fetch a goodly price. Fare you well."

Fully resuming my station and banishing all yearning of domestic bliss with a woman of unalloyed dedication to her husband's well-being, I recovered our horses while the maidens recovered theirs.

After the damsels had departed with their booty, I banished them from my thoughts with activity in aid of my master's comfort. In short order I prepared a poultice and dressed my master's wound, and we resumed our journey, as refreshed as we could be with only a brief respite from bloodshed and battle.

My master was lost in thought, which I wrongly imagined to be pain. "I know whence those knights came," he said with urgency.

"Then whence? Their weapons are not from this land, nor are they Moorish blades." I took up one of the swords, inspecting its distinctive gnarls and barbs, unknown to the smithies of the European continent. "Where were such as these forged?"

"In the East. These dark knights are enemies of our king, and they ride to Camelot. We must return thither to its defence straightway, ere it fall and our order with it."

I fastened the strange blade to my saddle. Who could know when it might be meet to use such a weapon?

Knowing where our duty lay, we spurred our horses on with urgency, in hope we would be swift enough, crossing hill and dale, rivers and reeds, moors and marshes. In the course of our journey we saw vistas we could not spare the time to enjoy. We saw injustices we could not spare to correct. We passed enemies we could not spare to discomfit. For if Camelot fell, all these would mean nothing.

In good time, though it seemed overlong, we crossed the tens of miles until we were rewarded with a view of Camelot, the splendour of which was marred with battle.

Resplendent with its towers and turrets, bastions and battlements, marble and granite, blood was even now being spilled, the verdant meadows surrounding the castle-city defiled with savage warfare. The hordes of dark knights fought to gain the city gates, but had not yet succeeded, held at bay by the King's mighty men of valour.

The herbs with which I had dressed my master's wound were potent, many of which were unobtainable in Britain, belonging to the mysteries of the East or of darkest Africa. He half-slept atop his mount, even as we had ridden at speed. In his stupefied state he could not wield a sword. I carried herbs which could have revived him—indeed, could have given him fresh vigour and freedom from pain. But his strength and agility would be nevertheless impaired, and I deemed it better—having witnessed him fight in the service of his king many times—to accept his place in this battle. My doubts as to the rightness of this choice duly acknowledged and ignored, I left my master invisible in the shadows and went forth.

If ever there were a time to trust my training, it was now. Without Sir Hudson's orders I rode hard to join the fray, my sword held at the ready. My master's comrades in arms, the Knights of the Round Table, fought valiantly as they shouted orders to their squires and to the foot soldiers. I was unique on the battlefield in fighting alone, having neither master nor Squire. The dark knights outnumbered ours threefold, but the king's mighty men diminished their numbers slowly albeit surely. Though hopelessly outnumbered, the King's forces fought the good fight, prevailing.

Joining the battle, I did my best to hold my own and deprive as many dark knights as possible of their lives. Only fleetingly did I feel the nakedness of being without my master, who had ever been my shield and defender in past conflicts.

My full attention occupied by the battle, I witnessed many things on that field. Such were the unspeakable acts of valour our King inspired that one could not easily distinguish oneself nor appear exceptional in battle among even the foot soldiers, for all the King's men fought as though their lives meant nothing as they smote the dark knights in their hundreds—and yet their skill was such that they were preserved.

One giant of a man, a full head greater in stature than any other, wielded an axe, and bore numerous deep arrow wounds, the shafts broken off near his skin. He was garbed little other than blood, most of which ran from his own wounds. Surely near death, he yet fought against our knights like a madman. Several dismembered bodies lay at his feet, while three knights of Camelot fought against him, evading his axe swings acrobatically while failing to do him enough harm to fell him.

As the battle progressed my horse was increasingly in danger of losing its footing among the bodies and bloody entrails. Many of those corpses had been laid there by my own sword. I had, in truth, cut down my share of dark knights this day—nay, more than my share, even having come late to the battle.

My blood ran cold when I saw, not far from me, the King, whom I had never before seen in battle. Should he not have been in his tower, and trusting his knights to prosecute the battle with success? Should he not have remained safe? Yet his presence on the field of battle inspired us all, from the least to the greatest.

An impressive figure with a well-groomed ginger moustache adorning his regal visage, he bore his armour lightly, without effort. He sat astride his horse, atop a grassy rise unsullied with the bodies of the dead, alone save for five dark knights against whom he wielded Excalibur with consummate skill.

Manifestly, the King needed none of my help. Indeed, it were more reasonable to expect him to come to my aid than the reverse.

But three more dark knights broke away from the main battle to join the assault on King Arthur, meaning to beleaguer him beyond the point of breaking. Closer to the King than any other of his warriors, my moorish horse and I sped to meet his foes, quickly closing the distance to smite the three dark knights ere they reached the king.

When King Arthur had dispatched the five dark knights with whom he fought, leaving them unmourned in bloody heaps, he looked at me—the King looked at me!—with recognition and nodded his gratitude.

Had I distinguished myself? The King had acknowledged me!

Then—how I had failed to see them before, I know not—two more dark riders appeared, almost as if materialising from the ether.

"Sire! Behind thee!" I cried out in alarm, already impelling my exhausted beast forward, vainly diminishing the distance between us.

The king spun round in response to meet his enemy, his sword flashing to kill the first dark knight, the legendary weapon plunging hilt-deep into the malefactor's armour and out the other side with a liberal lashing of blood.

But before he could withdraw his sword from the limp dark knight the Madman—appearing from I know not where—was upon him, demanding the King's life with the edge of his axe.

I was not close enough to defend the king. My arm would have needed to be much longer than it was. Unless—

Gripping my sword as the savage races grip a spear, I let it fly. My sword, flying true, pierced the chest of the Madman, fastening him with a deep thump to a tree behind him. He flailed his limbs, unable otherwise to move. I had done it. The life of my king was preserved, and I had done it.

His tired steed showing no sign of fatigue, my king closed the distance between us, smiling his Regal and—unbelievably—grateful smile, and took my hand. "My thanks, good squire."

In awe and disbelief of my sovereign's acknowledgement of his debt to me, I could only say, "My liege."

King Arthur surveyed the scene with dawning realisation of the price that had been paid for our victory—by our enemies.

Not one dark knight was left alive, yet our forces had suffered comparatively few losses. Our numbers were yet strong—scarcely diminished. Arthur's kingdom was yet triumphant.

The king held Excalibur high, the notable sword commanding the attention as effectively as the King's own standard. "Noble knights of the table round," King Arthur shouted. Done with their work, his knights quickly gathered around him from all parts of the battlefield, their enthusiasm for their king undiminished by the deluge of death all around them.

"This day we have won a great victory against our enemy, and for that I thank you all. Forsooth, your bravery is unequaled in all the world. We have made many widows this day!" The men unanimously shouted their approval. As for myself, I doubted whether any of the dark knights sported a wedding band. I had learned how six of them had treated two women, and I have no doubt that the knights were all cut from the same cloth. But the King continued his oration. "Presently we will witness the induction of another courageous knight into the court of Camelot. The squire of Sir Hudson hath shown his bravery in combat, and saved the life of his king."

Not only the knights, but the other squires and a multitude of foot soldiers, together with the common people who had been filtering out of the gates of Camelot unnoticed, cheered in ecstasy. It had been enough that the battle was won, the enemy vanquished, Camelot's kingdom saved from those who would do it harm and enslave it. But that they all were looking toward me as the object of their pleasure, I could not credit.

"He will begin the trials of knighthood on the morrow." The King came alongside me and clapped me on the shoulder, the golden glove of his armour ringing against the tarnished tin of my spaulder. I was not a small man at that time, but Arthur, King of the Britons, seemed to tower over me. Indeed, he good-naturedly dominated all with whom he stood. He raised his voice, manipulating the crowd. "But now, let us return to the castle and partake of meat and wine."

If it were possible, the din of cheers and shouts was louder this time than previously.

Soon, we were in the cavernous dining hall of Camelot, seemingly large enough to accommodate the entire kingdom. And all the kingdom was represented—not only the knights and nobles, but a multitude of commoners, invited by lottery to share the banquet with their king in his victory. The lavishly decorated room hosted an equally lavish spread of meats, fruits, vegetables, breads, deserts exotic and domestic, beer, wine, ales, and spirits—enough to satiate the appetite of the hungriest knights in the kingdom. And they—together with the common fighting men, publicans, blacksmiths, farmers, and all their wives—were waited upon by buxom serving wenches who refilled their plates and flagons with a liberality only possible with royal resources. Men were eating, men were drinking, men were drunk, but manners remained civilised. None fought, none raised a harsh word, none took liberties.

My master and I were seated together at the king's table, where only the sovereign and his special favourites of the day could join in exalted communion, commanding the best view of the happy chaos before us.

"I am proud for thee, my squire," Sir Hudson said to me as he gripped me on the shoulder. "As my act of bravery was rewarded, so shall thine."

"No bravery, master. The king's life is of greater value than my own," I said, meaning each word. "Any other would have done the same."

"But none other could have done so," my master said, a twinkle in his eye. "You thought I slept, that your potions and poultices had darkened my eyes. But there was light enough in them to see the battle though I could not engage in it." He chuckled, speaking to me as my friend rather than my master. "You pinned the King's enemy to a tree! With a mere throw! Of your sword! Most could not have done it with a javelin." He reclined in his chair, taking up his flagon before resting his feet on the table. Where were his encouragements to humility now? "Now eat, drink, and be merry, for tomorrow the king testeth thee."

Sir Hudson put a flagon of ale to his lips and drank deep and long.

I ate—indeed, one would think I had never seen victuals before—but I left my flagon untouched.

"Good man. Save the ale for after the trials. And while thou art being tested, I shall be thy squire."

Sir Hudson hunched forward to put down his flagon and leaned back in his chair.

Enjoying our place at the table for some hours more, we watched the others enjoy themselves as night turned to morning and vigour was diminished. We exchanged small talk and discussion of the day's battle with the king and his other favourites. I now moved in exalted circles previously denied me by court custom and protocol—traditions which I must soon swear to uphold even to death.

Tomorrow came quickly, with fanfare. In a heartbeat I was on the jousting field, heralded, armoured and mounted.

Sir Hudson stood beside me, as good as his word, divested of his armour and insignia. Wearing instead the tabard of a squire, he held my helmet and lance.

Having nothing further to teach me, my master offered me no advice as he handed me my weapons, except to bid me Godspeed.

Now properly equipped, I waited astride the horse that had been with me through so much from Moorish Spain and back to Christian England.

The trumpet blew. I dug my heels into the animal's loins and my horse launched toward my opponent who was also charging toward me at speed.

We rode to the thunder of hoofbeats and the roar of an appreciative crowd as we closed the distance between us. The joust bore little semblance to anything employed on the field of battle, but I eyed my opponent as if it did.

A subtle dodge at the last instant, a desperate parry, an artful lunge, enabled me to avoid the point of his lance, while mine splintered on impact with his armour and carried him off of his horse to an uncomfortable landing. I wanted to inquire after him whether he was unhurt, but there was no time ere I was carried away to my next test.

On my feet in a small round arena, armed only with a sword, I contended for my life, prevailing against a new contestant. The precepts permitted of no death blows, but I took pains to avoid even his hurt.

Shortly thereafter, with scarcely a transition, I was again on horseback, navigating an assault course at speed, demonstrating my horsemanship in jumping, dressage, and trick riding.

In an archery contest, I displayed my best shooting, scoring one bull's-eye after another, splitting arrows, and shooting apples from heads.

In unarmed combat with a man twice my size, I used his bulk and my agility to good advantage, having him bruised and bloodied while I remained relatively unscathed, finally pinning him to the floor—to the approval of my friends and those unknown to me.

Having tested me for the better part of the day in a variety of trials, and found me in no way wanting, I was brought before the king in the vast banqueting hall, now cleared of tables and revellers. It was crowded instead with a well-behaved and well-dressed cross-section of the great and the good from around the kingdom, standing in ranks according to their stations in the court.

Kneeling before Arthur on a raised dais, all eyes were upon us as I waited for him to speak. In my nerves and palpitations, I fought to keep from visibly shaking and weeping with pleasure.

"This boy—rather, this man," the King said in his dulcet voice loudly enough for all to hear, "hath passed all the tests of knighthood. Today Donovan Stone becometh a knight of the table round!"

While not anarchic, the crowd's cheering was enthusiastic. This throng hoped for and supported the advancement of a mere commoner—for some of them, one of their own—to the stellar heights of nobility, the sovereign's own inner circle.

My knees ached, and I dared not raise my head to look any higher than King Arthur's greaves. Every groove of his armour shone, freshly buffed and polished for the occasion.

But I had to look up at my king's face as he removed Excalibur from its scabbard and held it above me. He kept it there, protocol requiring him to intone the proper words before touching it to my shoulder.

"By the authority vested in me by the Almighty himself, I now dub thee Sir—"

A powerful but strained groan thundered from my left. I looked, and there was the Madman, broken chains dragging from the shackles decorating his wrists, rushing at me with his fists poised and slaughter in his eyes. Stumps of arrows still protruding from his flesh in half a dozen vital places, he left a trail of blood and sweat behind him.

A deafening klaxon intruded on my awareness with an obnoxious grind. The scene darkened and faded as I lost my discernment of the real and the less than real.

Chapter 5 – Further Out

You bring your fist down on the snooze button to try and stop the terrible—no, offensive—noise. The sound keeps coming—the grating urgent ringing sound. You bang on it a few more times, but it doesn't stop. The crack gets longer, nearer to the point at which it's going to break apart and hurt your hand.

It's not the alarm. Where is the telephone? Of course, it's exactly where it belongs, in its charging cradle.

Feeling in the dark, you locate the phone on the bedside table opposite the alarm clock. You pick it up. Thankfully, the ringing stops as you struggle in your sleepiness to figure out which way up it goes.

Barely conscious, but aware enough to know that you're not dreaming any more, you say only, "Hmm?"

You listen to the voice on the telephone.

"Of course," you say, your awareness returning rapidly, "I'm always up at this time."

You look at your bruised and battered but nevertheless faithful digital alarm clock, which is flashing 12:00. Perhaps it's not so faithful after all.

"What time is it?" you ask, rubbing your eyes with your free hand as you wait for an answer. "I'll be right there."

You hang up the phone, gather your strength, and roll out of bed. You stroke your chin with your fingers. Along with getting dressed and slapping on some cologne, you decide you need a shave. You need to be as tidy as your room.

Your fresh shave, combed hair, sharp suit, and brightly coloured tie beam confidence.

You are, at least in appearance if not in any other way, ready for the new day.

The drive to work doesn't take long. After parking outside the station in one of the usual inconvenient places, you go inside.

You're buzzed through the security door into the building, like any normal cop. Dave is loitering near the door. He could almost have been waiting for you. Unlikely though, since he wouldn't have known that you were coming.

"Hi, Don," Dave says, already sounding sympathetic. "I thought you were suspended for a while."

"Yeah, but King Arthur just called me in," you say, failing to even look at Dave as you begin walking down the corridor. "He's probably going to admit his mistake."

"Oh," Dave says, taking a breath or two in the meantime. "So how was the drive today?"

"Well, I didn't waste any breath shouting and swearing at the other drivers who got in my way, cut me off, and took no thought for the rules of the road, if that's what you mean. If I was still in possession of my badge, I'd've had them. But maybe, before the morning's out I'll possess it again."

"That's odd, for you to be so optimistic." Dave looks just a tad troubled.

Things suddenly look a little different. You stop walking, angling your head slightly and looking off into the busy corridor at nothing in particular. And nothing in particular looks right back at you.

"Do you know something I don't?"

"No, it's just strange," Dave says. "You're usually so... well, you're just not like that."

You resume walking, more slowly this time.

"Don't look so drained," Dave says.

"No. I've got nothing to be ashamed of."

"Of course not. Self-justification has never been your problem."

Dave wishes you luck and leaves you before you arrive at the Superintendent's door, ready—you think—to face him. True to form, you knock and enter.

Your heart sinks, and you get a bad feeling as you see a copy of that gutter press rag The Oracle on Superintendent Arthur's messy desktop. For his own good, you feel an urge to push all the junk off his desk.

"Come in. Ah. You already have."

"Have you read the paper today? Oh, I was forgetting. You don't read the papers. Just look at the pictures then." Arthur gestures to the tabloid, breaking a slight smile.

Unfolding the newspaper, you see the front page in all its glory. Justifying yourself now might be a bit of a problem.

You had forgotten about yesterday for some reason, but the paper reminds you. A large picture of yourself punching Lawrence Murphy takes pride of place on the front page. It even looks as though there's a spray of blood flying through the air in the photograph, which you have no doubt was added afterward. It enhances the satisfaction you felt at the time. Why in the world would you ever want to put that out of your mind?

A large headline above the photograph reads "City Cop Goes Crazy".

"Good action shot," you say. "Nice picture of me, but not a very flattering one of Murphy. What do you think, sir?"

Arthur's face reddens. Looking ready to explode, he keeps his voice calm but quavering. "Oh, it's wonderful. And get a load of the headline above it."

You comment, "It should say, 'Cop Cleans Up City'."

"It should say, 'Cop Gets Himself Fired'!"

You look up from the paper in semi-disbelief. "What did you say?"

"You heard me. You're not suspended anymore." A ghost of a smile crossed his lips, and the redness faded. "You're sacked. The taxpayers pay your salary, and they think you're a threat to them. I know you're a threat to us."

"Have you ever fired anyone from the force for bad PR before?"

"Your final pay is waiting for you," King Arthur said, the smile now breaking forcefully. "Go spend it."

"Sir, I just want you to know... you don't measure up to your namesake. I look forward to never working with you again."

You exit Superintendent Arthur's office without looking at him or waiting for any kind of reply, though you imagine the redness rising again.

Surprisingly, you find a small crowd of your colleagues—well, former colleagues—waiting outside the Superintendent's office, like a kettle of vultures. It doesn't occur to you that they might be waiting there to sympathise with you or congratulate you. With what would they be here to sympathise? Were you the last to find out?

You sneer at them, responding to their concern with a look that could melt iron.

Most of them scatter, skulking back to their proper posts, looking sympathetic but disappointed.

Bert and Dave, however, stay.

"I'm sorry about the bad news, Don," Dave says.

"Yes, I thought everyone might have known before I did," you say as you begin walking. "Who cares? That's the way the world crumbles."

Ever infuriatingly helpful, Dave says, "That's a mixed metaphor."

"No, it isn't," you reply.

"Don," Bert says, "if it helps at all, I think it's fantastic how you flattened that so-called reporter."

"It doesn't."

"Well, anyway, if there's anything I can do..."

"There isn't."

You pick up your pace and leave them behind.

There's only one more stop, one little errand, before you leave.

In various stages of dress and undress the male police officers, who had been chatting and joking with one another until you entered the room, silence themselves and stand by their lockers and look at you.

Finding your locker, you open it up and check whether there's anything in it you need to take home. Badge, truncheon, weapon. Otherwise empty. Nothing to take home. You turn and make for the door.

The armourer enters the locker room and makes for you.

"Hello Luke. Let me guess, the un-returned gun in my locker is a big no-no."

"I didn't even have to compare the gun's serial number with my records," Luke said, "to know who had failed to return it."

"That must give extra ammunition—no pun intended—to King Arthur's case against me. An irresponsible officer who upsets the press and fails to account for his weapon—never mind that he always gets his man."

"Yeah," Luke mutters.

"Here's your Glock. Now perhaps you'll go away."

Luke takes it, but he doesn't leave.

You head for the door. On your way out your colleagues ad-lib their goodbyes and farewells, their sympathies and commiserations, which you scarcely hear. You notice this one's locker has photos of his wife and kids stuck inside the door, and that one's locker contains photos of his girlfriend. Another's locker contains a Saint Christopher and photos of women the man probably would like to be his girlfriend. Still another has photos of his dog in his locker. Some have food and drinks, others good luck charms, others several changes of clothes.

"Don't you have homes? What's the point of filling up your locker, when the whims of your superior officer can take it all away just like that?"

Most of the officers hold out their hands to shake. You ignore them all. They speak words of encouragement or farewells, but you merely keep walking.

You leave the building and get in your car. You go through the motions of starting your engine, backing out of your parking space, and approaching the street, before you look both ways, and merge with traffic.

Then, seemingly without transition, you're approaching your house.

Unusually for you, you can't remember any part of the drive home. The familiar landmarks, the traffic lights always on red as you get to them, the pushy and inconsiderate traffic—it's all a complete blank.

You park on your drive, switch off the engine, stare out the windscreen at nothing, and realise you've sat in the car wasting several minutes of your allegedly valuable time. You open the door and get out of your car. Looking down at the open car door as you stand there with your unravelling maze of thoughts, you feel an inexplicable temptation.

You kick the door shut—hard. You find the noise as it slams strangely satisfying, as well as the dent left by your heel.

When you enter your house, you again slam the door behind you and survey the room, preparing to relax.

The living room is just as it always was in your previous life. You've done nothing to it except maintain it, as with the rest of the house, enshrining the memories it contains. The living room is clean and tidy, so there is no obstruction to flopping down in your most comfortable chair and putting your feet up on the pouffe with a heavy sigh.

Here too, vintage movie posters stand sentinel over your living space, enshrining what used to be your favourite hobby, and second favourite marital activity. Connery's James Bond embraces an initially unwilling Pussy Galore in "Goldfinger", possibly the best Bond movie ever. Another stylised 1960s poster hangs nearby, a yellow throng of soldiers advancing below a dark blue sky on "The Longest Day". From behind glass Humphrey Bogart sports his signature fedora, Walter Huston and Tim Holt keeping a careful eye on him as he surveys your living room, in "The Treasure of the Sierra Madre". Your neglected hobby: maybe you should take them down. But not right now.

You look at the telephone, mulling over the possibilities, and it seems to look back at you with unrealised potential.

Should you or shouldn't you?

Weighing up the possibilities, you decide you should. What's the worst that can happen?

You pick up the phone, considering that the worst that can happen is she can say no, and you dial the number.

The quiet electronic chirping representing the ringing at the other end of the line means you're committed. You take a deep breath.

"Hello, Jessica. I know you're probably still suffering from jet lag, but could I impose on you to take me out to dinner tonight?"

"Hmm. Obviously I'd love to," Jessica says, "but for two little difficulties. I'm broke, and I don't have a car."

"Don't worry, I'll pay and I'll drive."

"Aha. That's my favourite way to take someone out."

"Good. How does seven o'clock sound?"

"Make it seven fifteen, and you're on."

"All right, see you then. Good bye."

If that wasn't so hard, one would never guess it from your quaking hand. It was easier for you to shoot a man. Why should it be? You are only phoning your friend.

You fling the cordless phone across the room. It crashes into the wall just below Hildebrandt's fanciful "Star Wars" teaser poster. Apart from the thud, you hear a broken shard of plastic clatter away against the furniture, under the always watchful eyes of Luke Skywalker and Princess Leia.

Wondering what to do for the rest of the day, you look at your watch. Has the morning gone already? What a waste.

You lean back, rest your head, and wish you could take a nap. But you can never sleep in the afternoon. So you recline, close your eyes, and think. Not good.

Thinking was a good idea after all. Your mind turned to wondering about how Inspector Hudson was doing, and after a short drive you now find yourself in the hospital.

"Follow this corridor to the end, turn left, and you'll come to ward fourteen." The nurse alternates between pointing the way and looking at her computer screen. The nurses' station is messy, but there's nothing you can do about that. "Walk all the way through it until you come to fifteen. One of the ward sisters will tell you where Inspector Hudson's bed is."

You walk, in compliance with her directions.

"You're welcome, Constable Stone," she says to your back.

"Inspector," you correct her. "Mister," you correct yourself.

The endless corridors of the metropolitan hospital are well known to you, but you proceed according to the directions anyway. The corridor, the turn, then ward fourteen, pass you by. The absence of nurses on ward fifteen means you have to search for Hudson yourself.

You find him in a small private room. He's reading a magazine.

After stepping into his room and going unnoticed, you clear your throat.

"Don," he says with a note of surprise. "To what do I owe this pleasure?"

"Is it such a shock?"

"Well, you haven't visited me in two—" Hudson stops himself. "Well, in quite a while. Not even the other times I was in hospital. So like I said, to what do I owe the pleasure of your company?"

You take a seat at his bedside. "I was worried about you. I wanted to see how you're doing."

Hudson turns his head slightly away and looks at you obliquely. "Oh—kay. I'm doing well. The doc says I'll be out of here in a few days. But I'll be eating morphine for breakfast for a while."

You take a notebook and pen out of your inside coat pocket as you take up a businesslike posture. "What did you make of the weapons?"

Hudson blinks, shakes his head, and holds up his hands. "Weapons?" Then his face changes with his dawning comprehension. "Oh, so that's what this is about. Thanks for being so concerned about me. No really, I'm fine. Just a couple of organs damaged. Maybe only desk duty for me from now on."

Firmly, you say, "The weapons."

Hudson sighs with fatigue. "Okay. The weapons. Shiny military grade assault rifles. Heavy calibre pistols with laser sights. Stuff that's not available in this country. Not legally, that is. It's a puzzle. Where did they get that kind of ordinance?"

You rub your eyes. You scribble a little bit in your notebook while you read that one word written on the page.

"The… er…." Dare you tell him? A suspicion you got from a dream? "The Madman."

"No way," Hudson says with a grin. "A few no-hope scallies could never afford to pay the Madman's rates."

"What do you mean, scallies?"

"You know, wannabe criminal posers. People who spend what little money they have on beer, cigarettes, and looking like thugs. Not the kind of people who can afford to pay a black market luxury arms dealer."

"All I know about these thugs," you say, "is that they claimed to be demonstrating as part of some weird social justice jihad."

"What I'm more interested in," Hudson says, "is their van. It was vintage. Pre-war butcher's van. Dad's Army surplus. Pretty nicely scrubbed up too. Not a mark on it. A classic vehicle like that is arguably more expensive than their luxury weapons."

"So our late impoverished scallies were funded. Where did their money come from?"

"I don't know," Hudson says, his pupils suddenly dilated, "but get those spiders out of your hair." Hudson's gaze moves from the top of your head along an invisible line to the ceiling, where he follows the progress of something scary that only he can see as it inches along the ceiling until it's above his bed.

You get out of your chair and head into the corridor. Why is a nurse nowhere to be found?

"Sister," you shout down the corridor to a distant figure. She looks at you and begins walking in your direction. "Morphine reaction!" You point to Hudson's room.

You have a previous engagement, so you leave the medical professionals to their jobs.

Sweating, you knock at Jessica's front door. Why so nervous? You're simply going out for a meal with an old friend.

As you regain your composure, Jessica opens the door, looking relaxed and wonderful as ever.

"Hi," you say, manfully appearing equally relaxed. "Ready to go?"

"Yes," Jessica says with a smile which puts you genuinely at your ease. She turns to shout into the house, "I'm going now, grandma! Goodnight!"

Jessica closes the door behind her and locks it securely. You escort her to your car without touching her.

"I assume you read the news today," you say. You might as well get it over and done with now rather than later.

"Yes I did," Jessica says, indignant. She looks at you so as to hit you with the full force of her schoolteacherly sternness. "How could you do something like that? Beating up a reporter. What's the matter with you? You should be ashamed of yourself."

You open the car door for her, and she gets in. "I am. I just didn't realise how stupid it was until after it happened," you say. Jessica folds her arms across her chest and frowns.

You shut the door for Jessica—chivalry must be maintained—and then get in the car yourself.

Jessica is fastening her seat belt. "It wasn't just stupid. It was wrong," she says as she clicks the buckle home and points the finger. "I hope you realised that, too."

The modest engine comes to life as you turn the key and give it some gas. It roars in its modest, quiet, well maintained way.

"Yes, I did," you say, enduring, and perhaps enjoying, your whipping. Why not? You've got it coming. "You're right. Anyway, I got my reward. They gave me the sack."

You remember a proverb: Faithful are the wounds of a friend.

You drive off into the evening, into its promises and threats.

"I'm sorry."

"Sorry for telling me off? Or sorry I lost my job?"

"Really, you did deserve it. You'd better learn to control that temper."

"I do control it. I have been for a long time. If you only knew the half of it…"

"I mean it, Donovan," Jessica said, not allowing you to justify yourself. "How can you be so nasty to people sometimes? There's just no excuse for that." And then she erases her frown, just like that.

"So, what are you going to do now?" she asks, with some authority.

"Look for a job." It's a statement, but you inflect it as a question, like a kid who is probing his teacher whether he's got the right answer.

"Good. You're going to do that tomorrow, right?"

"Slow down. Tomorrow is my first day of unemployment. Shouldn't I have a cooling-off period or something?"

"Certainly not," Jessica commands, disallowing any objection or weakness. "You fall down," she makes corresponding gestures with her hands, "you get back up. Tomorrow. Right?"

You stare her down for as long as you can keep your eyes off the road, which you know annoys her safety conscious sensibilities to no end. "Riiiight."

"And you'll find one."

"Thank you for the vote of confidence."

You arrive at one of Jessica's favourite places, a gastropub in the heart of the city. "We've been here together a few times in the past two years," she says.

"Which is something when you consider that you're only in town during Christmas and summer holidays," you say.

Your conversation pauses as you enter the restaurant and are seated.

After a few minutes of perusing the familiar menu in comfortable silence, you summon the waiter over to take your order.

The waiter approaches and stands by your table, his pad and pencil at the ready. "Are you ready to order?"

"I'll have the chargrilled steak," you say.

"Yes sir. How would you like the steak done?"

"On the grill, of course."

"Just give it to him well done," an embarrassed Jessica says.

"And what kind of potatoes would you like?"

"Jacket."

"Ooooh-kay," the waiter says. "Do you want anything on that?"

"A skin."

"Donovaaaaan…" Jessica rebukes.

The waiter eyes you strangely. "Yes, sir. And for you miss?"

"I'd like the rib-eye steak with chips—ooh, I really shouldn't order that—and green salad." Jessica makes eye contact with the waiter. "By the way, please forgive my friend. All the other waiting staff here have refused to serve him again."

"That's alright," he says. "I'm new here. And how would you like the steak done?"

"Medium."

"And to drink?"

"Coke and rum," you say.

"Make that two cokes." Jessica corrects your mistake.

The waiter looks to you for approval, more wary of finding himself on your bad side than on hers.

"You heard the lady."

"Fine. I'll be right back with your drinks."

The waiter leaves, heading for the kitchen.

"Now what were we talking about," you say, fidgeting with the napkin and cutlery, "before we were so rudely interrupted?"

"You were about to tell me what's on your mind," Jessica says, sitting back and relaxing in her chair.

"Well," you say as you shuffle about, "I don't remember promising that. Anyway… it's nothing, really. I just wanted to spend some time with you."

"Let's make it some quality time then. Tell me what's gone on in your life while I've been away, aside from what you've already told me."

You pause. "Nothing really."

"Nothing at all?"

"Well… I've been having a lot of dreams."

"Tell me about them."

"They're very vivid… and good." You laugh to yourself. "Better than life."

"Donovan, you can get a hold of your life. Reality is more important than dreams."

"Reality!" you laugh. "Life is just a psychotic nightmare. What do I want with reality?"

"How can it really be that bad?" Jessica leans forward, putting her elbows on the table.

"It just is. My dreams sort of make up for it," you say as you shrug. "They make me happy."

"Well, at least it's good to know there's one thing that makes you happy," Jessica says, half smiling.

"Two things, actually."

"Oh yes? What's the other one?"

The answer doesn't require any thought. "You are, of course."

Jessica smiles and blushes. "Oh. Thank you." She looks away, tapping her fingers on the table. "So, when was the last time you had one of these dreams?"

"Last night."

"And what was it about?"

"It was about…" you pause to think, finding you can't remember the specifics. "It was about… something I want, and can't have. That is, something I can't have here, in reality. But in the dream I can have it. Except that it disappears at the last second, when my alarm goes. Always an instant before I can claim whatever it is."

"That must be frustrating," Jessica says.

You shake your head and grin. "They're only dreams."

The evening has passed much too quickly, seemingly in a heartbeat. You park your car in front of Jessica's house, participating uncomplainingly in the chivalrous ritual that requires you open the door for her to let her out and then close it behind her. It's a silly ritual, but you put up with it without knowing why.

Your duty of gallantry discharged, you walk to the front door and then wait as she fumbles through her handbag for her keys before unlocking the door. She opens it, sighs, and says, "I suppose you'd like to come in."

"Yes, but I can only stay a few hours," you say with a grin.

Jessica laughs. "Try a few minutes. I'm tired."

"I'll take what I can get."

The two of you enter the house. It's getting cold outside, and you're glad of the exaggeratedly warm temperature Jessica's grandma maintains in her house. Jessica flicks on a couple of lights to bathe the living room in a comfortable glow to complement the warm temperature.

It's a modest front room with barely enough space for the three-piece suite and upright piano it contains. It's comfortable though, having the somewhat out of date furniture and decor that is usually found in an old person's home, coupled with the immaculate cleanness that a conscientious retired person maintains. The exception is the corner where Jessica throws down all her stuff.

"Sit down, Donovan."

You comply willingly, taking a relaxing seat on the sofa while Jessica makes herself comfortable on the chair.

"Have you been practicing while you've been away?"

"A little," she says, hesitating.

"So are you going to play something for me this time?"

"Okay." Jessica makes a show of sighing deeply and standing up with mock weariness before sitting down again in front of the piano. She interlocks her fingers and makes a show of stretching them out in front of her, allowing a few pops to sound from her knuckles. She begins to play. "If you'd like something to drink, try the fridge."

"All right," you say. "Do you want anything?"

"No, thank you."

You enter the kitchen, also immaculately clean while being about twenty years out of date, and open the refrigerator. You survey the drink situation, simultaneously pleased and disappointed. Alcohol of any kind is conspicuous by its absence. There are fruit juices and bottled water. It looks like your choice has been made for you.

You remove a carton of orange juice. Grandma always keeps the best and most expensive brand in her fridge, which, on her budget, makes you wonder how she can afford it. As you fill your glass you hear the alluring strains of classical piano music, relaxing you. Even though you hardly ever see this place, you feel at home here.

You follow the soothing sound to stand next to the slightly out of tune piano, hovering like a music teacher as Jessica plays. Her grandma doesn't play, only keeping the piano for Jessica, and might not be able to afford to have it tuned.

The music takes your breath away even as it relaxes you, lulling you away from the grotty world you inhabited as a cop. At this moment you're almost glad that you don't have to go back to it. Jessica, of course, insists that her playing is nothing special—she even considers it mediocre. You disagree, without being disagreeable.

The time melts away under Jessica's musical ministrations.

"I do enjoy playing," she says.

"And I enjoy being played to. It puts me in a different world. The wordless abstract fantasy of the music is a little like dreaming."

Jessica's hands slow slightly, creating an unscripted dissonance. "Don't you," she says haltingly, "have anyone else, Donovan?"

"No," is your curt reply.

"Why not?"

"It's not by choice. Not mine, anyway."

Jessica misses a note. "I can never get this piece right."

"Don't judge your entire performance on one note," you say. "But then I guess I've missed far more than just one proverbial note in my life. I'm tired, too. I think it's time I was going."

Jessica rises with visible relief as she shakes the musical strain out of her fingers. She sees you to the door and opens it for you.

"Thank you for the dinner," she says, as she warmly hugs you. "I had a very nice time."

"Thank you for taking me. See you later." You turn to go, waving over your shoulder at her as she politely waits in the doorway.

You leave the house and get in your car, while she stands in the doorway, watching. She'll stay there until you're gone, waving you off. You wish she wouldn't, that she would go into the house instead and get in from the cold night air, but she won't be told.

You drive home, alone again.

After a day that was as short as it was long, you arrive home, stopping your car in the drive. The engine dies as you remove the key and get out of the car, closing the door behind you and noticing the dent you put there earlier in the day.

You move toward your front door, ready to get to bed and accept whatever surprises sleep holds for you tonight. But you hear a noise and stop to listen. You hear the sound of footsteps coming from the shadows.

A man emerges from the gloom—a man you recognise, whose photo was shown to you yesterday. The sodium street lighting and the light at your own front door illuminates him enough for you to identify him as Stephen Gates, out of prison and probably wanting some kind of revenge.

Gates has a hood over his head and a long handled garden implement in his hand. He swings the stick at you. You want to get in close to prevent him and wrestle him to the ground, but he's too quick. He hits you squarely on the head—not enough to stun you, but it hurts and you stumble to the ground.

As he raises the stick and prepares to strike you again, you kick his feet out from under him. He lands on his back, having his breath knocked out of him and giving you a chance to get up, though you find yourself a little unsteady on your feet.

You reach down to drag him up by the scruff of the neck and thump him once to keep him quiet.

Nearly motionless on the ground, Gates breathes and groans, signalling your victory. Wondering what your next move should be, you realise you are now eligible to call the police, entitled to the same level of protection as any other private citizen. Is the unconscious man lying in a heap on your lawn emergency enough to dial 999, or should you just call the local police station? If you'd had a chance to get to the phone you might have called, but you won't get the chance right now.

Another—previously unseen—man emerges from the shadows. He jumps you, knocking you down—now it's you who is winded. Gates is up on his feet again, not as unconscious as he seemed. Together, Gates and the unknown accomplice rain a hail of fists upon you. You curl up into a ball to minimise the damage. They bruise your back, ribs, and head—you think you hear a finger break, which serves them right—and you bear it, looking for your opportunity. Glancing left and right, but only slightly to avoid breaking your cover, you see the gardening tool that Gates has dropped, lying in the grass an arm's reach from you.

You grab it and emerge from your foetal position, lashing the long handle wildly in the direction of your two attackers, swinging it in anger as well as defence.

You score good hits on both of them, cracking one of them on the skull and the other—miraculously—in the groin. They flee, suddenly keen to get away from you.

Shaking with adrenaline, hurting, and weak in the knees, you collapse on your back into the wet grass. Catching your breath while you let your strength return, you remain lying on the ground for a few minutes.

You rise, soaked with sweat and with the moisture you absorbed from the wet ground. Gingerly, you move to the door and get your key out of your pocket, fumbling with it, first to find the right key on your ring of several, and next to fit it into the lock. This process seems to take a while, but it's probably only just a few seconds. You're still only just regaining your composure as you open the door and enter.

Once inside, you lock the door and drop your keys on the floor. You wonder if you should call the police. No, it's too late for them to help you. What you really need is to clean yourself up.

In the bathroom the mirror reveals the damage. Your face is marked and bloodied, inflicted with some new battle scars.

Your blood mixes with the tap water and goes down the drain in a pink flume as you wash your face with a warm wet towel. It soothes you a little. When you're cleaned up you see that the cuts are small and the bruises few. The bleeding has mostly stopped.

Drenched, soiled, and dirty in every other part, you have a languid shower before retiring, exhausted, to bed where sleep quickly consumes you.

Chapter 6 – 20,000 Yards Across the Frontier

The crops were razed to the ground. Fragments littered the fields.

There were no animals. Correction: some distance away, I saw one mutilated cow carcass.

The farm house was knocked over as if by a tornado, as were the corrals and stables.

There was a man watching me as I rode in slow on my appaloosa—the poor sodbuster who owned the place probably. He held a rifle loosely in the crook of his arm, pointed at the ground. Between him and me there was a well.

I swung my leg over my horse's head and slid off the saddle. My spurs jangled and a cloud of dust rose off my jeans as my feet touched the ground. My hat, coat, bed roll, horse—everything I owned in fact—was caked in dust and needed cleaning. My sixgun felt heavy at my hip, my hat felt heavy on my head, I was tired and thirsty. However, it was a blessed relief to be on my feet after a couple of days in the saddle.

Like I said, the well was between me and the sodbuster. I cranked the pulley to lower the bucket and fill it, then cranked it back up. I put the bucket to my lips and poured the crystal water into my mouth, drinking my fill for the first time since my canteen ran empty in the desert yesterday. My hat fell off my head and onto the ground as I drank. The water spilled over, running down my five-day stubble and turning the dust caked on my shoulders and chest into mud. I poured the rest of the bucket over my head, and then repeated the process a few times, giving myself a makeshift shower, clothes and all, until I had rinsed off most of the mud.

"Morning," I said, looking at the farmer, who still crooked his rifle at the ground. "What's up?" I asked, glancing around to indicate the havoc that used to be his farm.

The sodbuster opened his mouth and closed it again. Maybe he was traumatised, or maybe out of practice talking to people. He took a few breaths, beginning to form words and giving up on them like he wasn't sure where to start. "In the middle of the night... a mighty wind... swirlin' dust everywhere... noises, bangin' and creakin'... lights movin' all around... in the mornin' all the animals was gone. Ain't nothin' much left in the fields neither!"

"What was it?" I took in the devastated result of this... visitation. Even though I'd seen this before, I couldn't imagine what had done it, and the sodbuster's description of it didn't help form any kind of useful picture in my mind.

"You tell me, mister! Now goodbye. I'm ridin' East."

I put my sodden hat back on my head, and put my fingers to its brim. "Bon voyage."

Putting two fingers between his teeth and whistling, the sodbuster summoned his horse, an old grey nag which had seen better days but at least had not been collected or eviscerated by the visitor. He took hold of the saddle horn, got a foot in the stirrup, and wearily swung himself onto the beast's back. I heard the hoofbeats as he rode away, but I didn't watch him go. Something else caught my eye.

There were ruts in the ground, like wagon tracks only a lot wider. They crisscrossed the plain in all directions. The wheels must have carried many tons of weight to leave impressions this deep in such dry ground. There were several parallel sets of tracks, like the wagon that left them had a lot more than just four wheels. I looked around for a while longer, but didn't find anything else helpful except what I took to be more of these wheel traces heading out across the plain. I got back on my horse and rode off in their direction.

Night was beginning to fall, and I could see the glow of campfires in the distance. Night would be cold on the plain, and the warmth of a fire would benefit me to no end. I also thought I could hear injun drums sounding in the direction of the nearest campfire.

Hoping they were friendly injuns and not the ornery savages they often turned out to be when they met a white man with a pistol on his hip, I rode toward the fires.

It didn't take me long to reach their camp.

A group of braves sat around the fire, chattering in their savage tongue. There were no squaws or papooses, so it was probably a hunting party.

The injuns looked grim, on edge.

I could overhear their talk around the campfire. Lucky for me they were of the Meco tribe—I learned their savage chatter ten years ago when I was a cavalry scout, acting as a sort of unofficial ambassador between the white man and the red man. It didn't end well.

Rather than let on that I knew their lingo, I thought I'd see first if they spoke American. "Hi there."

One of the injuns stood up and came over to where I was still astride my horse.

"How," he said in cautious greeting.

"I don't know how. I've been trying to figure that out for years," I said.

Three of them stood up, raising their tomahawks threateningly, fear in their eyes and firelight on their faces.

"Sorry, I've been in the desert a long time and forgotten most of my manners," I said as the three approached me and my horse, joining their brother, "not that you redskins are too bothered about manners."

The braves dragged me off my horse and started pummelling me, not trying to kill me, but just making it hurt. Me and my big mouth.

One thing you can't do is show fear around these savages. They sense it like a wolf. I tried to put the pain out of my mind and talk to them through the punches, though I dearly wanted to hit them back. "Anyhow," I said while they continued to beat me, "I just want to ask you—ow!—about whatever's been—oof!—destroying crops and—ugh!—stealing livestock."

They stopped attacking me, and backed off. I was grateful.

They looked at each other, searching each other's faces for approval.

"Now come on, braves. I know you know something that can help me. I've seen your smoke signals puffing over the hills."

Speaking to me in their Meco tongue, their leader said, "Impossible. No white man understands our code."

"Hot air. I know your secret codes well enough. I'm a pretty clever guy when I want to be. But you weren't very specific in your warnings to your village."

They conferred quietly. Then each one told me what he had seen and heard.

"We have seen a ghostly juggernaut moving across the plains like the wind," the tall injun said.

"It has many wings!" the short one said.

"It glows like a thousand fireflies," the thin one said.

"It roars like stampeding buffalo," the musclebound one said.

I listened to them with great interest until I remembered I was still prone on the ground and hurting with bruises. I got up and started brushing the dust off my clothes, dry again after my ride through the arid landscape, and now dirty again to boot. "Which direction did it come from?" I asked.

In unison they all pointed north.

"Did it go back the same way?"

They all nodded.

"Thanks," I said. "You savages have been really helpful."

The injuns sneered and grunted, but let go the insult, knowing that the white man never really understood them.

Following the lead of my injun friends, I got back on my horse and made north, hurting but unhurt.

Sparing no time for sleep, I rode on through the bright moonlit night following the occasional wide ruts where the ground was soft enough for an impression to be left. Most of the sunbaked ground out in this part of the plain was like stone—only a bundle of TNT would make any impression on it until the floods came.

At about sunup I came across a group of cowpokes sitting around a campfire, eating breakfast, drinking coffee, and twittering like a gang of kids playing with a dead cat.

I swung myself down from the saddle and went over to the campfire like I was an honoured guest whom they had been expecting.

Taking a nearly clean tin mug and pouring myself some of their coffee, I pretended to enjoy the taste and aroma of the foul mixture.

"Any of you boys," I said, "know anything about what's been destroying crops and making livestock disappear?" They were inexperienced—none of them had ever heard of a poker face.

I looked around and surveyed the bulls and heifers making up their herd. Sealed with several different brands, they were well-fed and well-cared-for animals, a lot of money and attention having been spent on them, though these cowboys looked about as ill-favoured and unkempt as anyone I've seen on the plains.

"Why would we know anything about that?" one of the hands said.

Another of the cowboys spoke up. "We ain't seen no nothin' nor no body," he said, almost as if scripted and rehearsed, and poorly acted to boot. "These here is our cattle."

"Sorry boys." I bent over the campfire to light up a cigar—my first one in days. "I must be giving the wrong signals," I said apologetically before I stood up again, puffing on my cheroot. "I'm not trying to impugn your veracity."

The rustlers stood up. "You gonna do what to my velocity?"

I took a deep drag on my stogie, feeling its properties rush into my core.

Good hard experience is the best teacher, and one thing you know when you're an experienced gunfighter is when people are about to draw. They may do their best to look as cool and natural as at any other time, but if they're planning to kill a man then something happens to the stance, the expression, the breathing, and you can just tell. And these guys were about to draw.

Despite their numbers, I had the advantage. They couldn't have got that same kind of read on me, because I wasn't about to draw. Unless they drew first.

I took stock of them automatically. Seven men, all standing, all guilty as sin—of something, anything. Three of them were ready, just itching to kill as only true murderers are.

The three went for their guns as I watched them in bullet-time, so far ahead of them that I knew I needn't rush. Before they cleared leather I had put bullets through their heads, the slugs languidly emerging from the backs of their skulls with trails of blood and bone. The corpses took a couple of steps toward me before realising they were dead and falling over, striking the ground with a noise like—to my heightened senses—thunder.

The four remaining rustlers had their hands over their guns, weighing up. Would four of them have a chance where three had failed?

"You boys have a death wish too?" My gun was already out and ready. I holstered the weapon—fair play and all that.

"You'll be killed too," one of the rustlers said, a half smile curling his ugly lip. "You ain't got that many bullets left."

"You know, you may be right," I said. "I lost count. Feeling lucky?"

"Maybe," the rustler said.

The four rustlers went for their guns. They were no faster than the previous three—I had all the time in the world, but not enough bullets left in my six-shooter.

Diving to the ground, I rolled, and came up in a spot where the four men were stacked up from my line of sight in two rows of two. Like shooting turkeys, it almost seemed unfair as I fired two rounds, and all four men collapsed to the ground, without a word, without a gasp, just plain dead.

I had fooled myself in my euphoria—the four men weren't dead yet. But they were dying fast. I looked at the dying men and tried to work out which one would live for minutes rather than seconds.

I spoke to the one with the most life left in him, the one most likely to respond to my gentle appeal. "I hadn't really lost count you know. I've still got one shot left."

I knelt down next to him, demonstrating my best bedside manner, and made a show of pointing my gun at his knee, jabbing it with the barrel. He winced as he looked at it in fear.

"Now, you haven't got much longer to live. I could use this last bullet to make your last minutes a lot more painful." I tried to look sympathetic, and probably failed, as I moved my pistol to aim at his hideously ugly head. "Or I could use it to put you out of your misery quick. Now, I asked you a question, remember? About what's been destroying crops and making livestock disappear."

He didn't say anything right away, so I moved the gun barrel back down to his knee.

The dying man spoke, gasping. "Ghost ship... sailing the seas... no water..."

"You want water?"

"No water... no ocean... ghost ship... sailing—"

The rustler choked and sputtered, his life expiring. He breathed his last.

It looked like I got to keep my last bullet. Fine with me. I had a thing for conserving resources.

A little later that day, while the buzzards feasted on the cattle rustlers, a mighty wind blew across the plain, churning up the desert into a cloud of stinging dust.

Riding against the wind and unable to see, the roar was deafening, and the sand must have stung my poor old nag's eyes. But she kept going, indefatigable.

A few minutes passed, and the dust began to clear. The roar became quieter without fading entirely.

The dust storm receded toward the horizon, roiling like a cumulus cloud but centring around a particular area. I strained my eyes at the limits of their vision to penetrate the dense haze. I thought I could see, within the billowing dust, a shimmering body of water, a lazy lake just large enough to encompass the cloud. There were no lakes for a hundred miles in any direction according to my maps, and—having travelled this region before—I was inclined to trust them.

The obscuring dust began to clear as I watched. Emerging from it, sailing on the impossible lake, was a ship.

I dug my spurs into the loins of my unhappy beast, hopefully urging her on at a speed unsuited to her age for one last time, and rode in the direction of the sailing ship as fast as my animal could carry me. Always faithful, she obeyed me, carrying me forward to gain on the strange spectre. The closer I got to it the more it looked like a ship in full sail, catching even the highest wind with its moonrakers. It was making unwavering headway, its helmsman handling it well, moving much faster than any normal sailing ship. It could only have been a ghost ship.

As I neared the lake the shoreline receded away from me, enticing me with its nothingness, fooling my eyes just as similar illusions have fooled the eyes of countless unfortunate desert travellers over the centuries. But ocean vessels usually didn't figure into the typical wasteland mirage.

As my ungainly but tireless animal closed the distance, the vessel resolved itself more and more. It moved gracefully across the endless plains on massive wagon wheels. This ship was vast, much larger than most seagoing vessels, and flat-bottomed, giving the illusion of being half-immersed. Equipped with many billowing sails, glowing lamps, and an array of cannon, it kicked up a lot of spray as it rolled along the desert ground, perpetuating the dust storm that heralded the ship.

Ropes and riggings trailed from the vessel, madly dragging and bouncing along the ground. I let my horse have her head, and despite her fatigue she pelted at an amazing pace, turning yards into inches. The noise of the ship's metal-clad wheels was deafening even as I approached it.

The exhausted beast carried me underneath the ship, surely at the end of her endurance. I reached out for one of the ropes, lunging like a madman as I parted company with the saddle. My booted feet were dragged along in the thick dust of the desert floor.

My horse slowed down. Probably as relieved as any animal ever could be, she could rest now and I quickly lost sight of her as I climbed hand over hand, ascending ever closer to my goal. My arms were tested to breaking point—rope climbing was not my best skill—but I made progress.

I reached the railing, relieved in much the same way my appaloosa must have been, climbing up and over before collapsing in an exhausted heap on the deck. With difficulty I got to my feet, but the motion of the ship had me swaying like the town drunk.

Some of the ship's crew members, some uniformed like sailors and others costumed like pirates, approached me with swords in hand. Though it was futile, I drew my pistol and fired my one remaining bullet, failing to hit anyone or anything. I was accustomed to firing from solid ground or horseback, not the swaying deck of a bucking ship. I might have saved that bullet and made it count for something later. Chalk it up to experience which might be useful later in life—if my life had a later.

The sailors overpowered me and hustled me across the deck of the amazing ship, giving me a chance to dimly take in my surroundings and learn the lay of the land, so to speak. Battered, bruised, and barely conscious, my awareness of the room into which I was bundled was vague.

I was dropped onto a bed—a comfortable bed at that. Letting my eyes close, I lay there for I don't know how long, until I became aware of someone standing over me.

I also had the impression of others in the cramped cabin.

Forcing my eyes open, I saw the Captain, dressed in an immaculate seafarer's uniform. He seated himself in the chair opposite, crossing his legs and making himself comfortable while smoking an elegant European cigar.

"I don't know who you are, or why you're here," the Captain said, before inhaling a lungful of sweet smelling tobacco smoke. "But you must know that the only alternative I have to keeping you here is to kill you."

"Well, that would ruin my day," I said, sitting up in my bed and rubbing my eyes.

"Your droll tone suggests to me you are a man of courage and intelligence," the Captain said, letting smoke escape from his mouth and nostrils. "You have successfully sought me out on the plains while I use dust storms, night, isolation, and superstition to hide myself. I imagine you questioned people along the way, perhaps even killed them to find us. You have showed no fear in boarding the ship from your horse, even chasing us down in a sandstorm." He spoke with detached interest, certain I was no threat to him. "Just what is it you want from me?"

"I was sent by the government to solve the mystery—the stripped farms, the missing animals, the sodbusters left half insane," I said. "But, personally, I'm interested in what drives a man to do something like this." I raised my hands in the air and looked around, taking in not just the little room in which I was incarcerated, but the crew and the ship as a whole.

The Captain gestured his aides away, and they left the room. He stood up and looked down on me. "My ship is called the Sulinaut. It carries a crew of hundreds. Apart from needing to feed my crew, I ravage farms and drive sodbusters half insane for revenge against the society that has created me."

Allowing a laugh to escape my lips, I said, "So are you some kind of mad scientist then?"

Maintaining a pleasant tone, the Captain continued speaking. "I am prepared to trust you—to a point, that is. You may have the run of the ship, and so long as you do not interfere with my work or try to escape you may enjoy your freedom. There are many diversions you can enjoy, such as a games room, library, and other things." The Captain assumed a cautioning tone. "But beware: my crew are well-trained in oriental fighting techniques, and will have no trouble subduing or killing you.

"Yeah, your crew" I said. "How did you come by them? Trained landship seamen must be pretty thin on the ground nowadays."

"I picked these men up from the streets. I provide all their needs, train them, arm them, and give them an outlet for their restlessness and aggression. I am their benefactor. Some are farmers, others technicians, all are merciless killers at my command. Their lives are worth nothing, and they will joyfully stand in front of a gatling gun or go to the gallows for the sake of an opportunity to kill. Their greatest thrill in life is to use the power I afford them." The Captain gloated over the sway he held.

"Impressive." I couldn't think of anything else to say.

"Of course my great personal wealth also helps. And, no, you won't be able to trace it. I've taken care of that."

"Of course you'd cover your tracks," I said. "And you're probably not even known by name to any of your crew. I'll bet all the money you use for this enterprise is ensconced on this ship in the form of gold ingots, diamonds, or other untraceable commodities."

The Captain knocked on the door. A uniformed woman entered the room.

"My yeoman will show you to your cabin," the Captain said.

"My cabin? I assumed this would be my cabin."

"You can stay here if you want. This is the brig," the yeoman said. "This way please."

I rose, attempting to master my pain, and followed her.

The Captain crossed the deck, going about his business, entering a door that I assumed led to his cabin, while I began a brief tour of the Sulinaut. But it was cut short. As the yeoman escorted me across the deck I heard the sound of a naval whistle. The crew scrambled about in a flurry of activity.

The yeoman now looked misplaced. "I have to rejoin my shipmates. See that door there? That's your cabin," she said, pointing, and then rushed away, leaving me standing alone on deck while people moved in a frantic orderly chaos all around me.

The Captain burst out of his cabin, his face set with deadly seriousness. He made eye contact with me. "Mr Stone, you will now witness the business of this ship—in the first-person, so to speak." The Captain moved off at a sprint, deftly avoiding the others who were doing the same.

The ship was travelling through a vast farm. As the vessel turned hard I almost lost my footing, but I was getting my sea legs now. I followed the Captain all the way to the command centre. The ship's bridge was unlike anything I had seen in my extensive travels. There were rows of levers and banks of dials and, in addition to windows looking directly outside there were strange windows that showed views of other things—the outside, and other parts of the ship—not otherwise visible from here.

My acquaintance with machines was very limited. I didn't know what to make of all the gleaming brass and shining glass, magic windows and spinning wheels.

"Here we harness the power of the wind, Mr Stone. These controls give me the power to carry out my purposes. And these periscopic monitors," he said without looking away from whatever he was doing, "use a system of mirrors to show me other aspects of the ship. I can manage absolutely everything from right here." The Captain shouted orders I couldn't comprehend to several of the crew members manning the controls.

In the monitors I saw what appeared to be enormous scoops extending from the underside of the ship, preceded by complex wheels of knives and pins. The wheels stripped the ground of its crops without regard for what might get in the way, and the scoops collected the harvest. Another massive scoop collected the livestock, taking cattle, pigs, goats, and even horses.

Other monitors showed cavernous harvesting hoppers, where the collected crops and animals were deposited and dealt with by the Sulinaut's large and skilled crew. There was no doubt that the Captain was a talented inventor—this was a new method of farming which, if harnessed peacefully rather than in the mad desire for revenge, could revolutionise agriculture in every way.

The ship was consuming an entire farm, its diabolical passing marked by its table leavings.

Need I say that I was impressed? Amazed. But undeniably dubious.

Sensing my apprehension, the Captain turned to face me. He smiled, self-satisfied.

Forgetting I had no more bullets in my gun, I drew on the Captain.

Fast as a flash of lightning, the Captain disarmed me with a precise kick of his left foot, and followed up with his right, sending me tumbling backward to finish painfully on the wooden floor.

The searing pain and the impact left me unable to breathe. I had only ever seen Chinamen perform such moves before. I fancied my chances against him in the negative.

"I've never been the most moral of men, but what you're doing sickens me to the core," I said when breath came back to me. "I will stop you."

The Captain only smiled his proud smile at me.

The monitors got my attention as, the operation completed, the wheels and scoops retracted into the ship's underside. The Sulinaut shuddered and shook while the machinery drew the harvesting equipment up, and I lay transfixed by the view on the monitor.

One of the scoops was stuck, still skimming along the ground, juddering the entire ship.

A pack of wolves—there must have been hundreds of them—appeared in one of the monitors, running, doing their best to keep up with the Sulinaut. The ship was moving too fast for them and they were falling behind.

The crew on the bridge all fixed their eyes on the monitors, stopping everything to watch the wolves. To a man the sailors assumed an almost tangible foreboding.

"Nirewolves. Not again," the navigation officer intoned.

Even the Captain observed the wolves with a frown.

"What are Nirewolves? The land-ship equivalent of an albatross?" Nobody listened to me.

I expected the Captain to reassure his crew, to tell them there's no such thing as bad luck or bad omens. But he seemed the most affected, silent and sullen as he watched the creatures.

"Sir, we have a problem with scoop six," the First Officer said.

The Captain snapped out of his reverie. "See to it, Number One."

"Yes sir."

On one of the control banks, among the dizzying confusion of levers, stops, dials, and indicators, I could see a round gauge with a needle. Large enough to be seen from anywhere on the bridge, it displayed the ship's speed in knots. I could feel the difference as the needle began turning counterclockwise. We were losing speed.

The wind had been interrupted. I wasn't the only one who noticed. The crew members' dark foreboding turned to palpable alarm.

As the Sulinaut slowed, its sails slack, the animals were easily able to overtake it. They swarmed into the broken scoop.

In seconds the Nirewolves overran the deck, attacking everything and everyone, filling every part of the ship like a liquid. Crewmembers everywhere ran in terror, their oriental self defence useless against the frenzied animals.

Some of the crew did succeed—for a moment—in fighting the wolves off, using long handled tools, swords, and guns, but as the creatures emerged from every opening, the sailors were overwhelmed.

Resistance useless, the crew scattered, wisely running away from the problem rather than facing it head on.

Safe on the elevated bridge—so far—we were able to more calmly assess the situation as it developed. I watched the monitors intently. The crew in the harvesting rooms, who had been assigned to look after the newly collected livestock, had abandoned their posts—the wolves had entered there as well, worrying the cattle, which in turn followed their keepers and stampeded onto the deck looking for an escape.

When the cattle emerged from below decks they immediately did major damage, their weight exceeding the design specifications of the ship in every way as the herd spread out into parts of the vessel never made to carry that kind of load. Their feet made holes in the floor, and some of the animals simply fell through, while others butted up against walls and railings, breaking them beyond further usefulness.

The ship groaned under the wounds inflicted upon it by the frenzied livestock. As the damage became greater, some of the periscopic monitors stopped working, or simply showed images of splintered wood. But enough of them still functioned to give a good view of the mayhem overcoming the ship.

The animals were beginning to escape the vessel. Some fell through the holes in the floor, some went over the railings, and many of the Nirewolves made a bid for freedom by way of the damaged scoop.

Soon, the animal madness had ended, all the creatures having escaped the ship or died. Many of the crew members had also fled by now, some of whom I could see running into the distance away from the doomed Sulinaut. Others were trampled by stampeding cattle.

The ship began to buck and kick as the wind picked up again. Maybe its wheels were damaged—the Sulinaut moved erratically as it gained speed. The Captain was wrestling with the controls, his officers having abandoned him, when the turbulence caused him to fall and brought a section of the roof down on him, pinning him to the floor.

I went to him and lifted the wreckage from him. A broken piece of planking was piercing him through the gut.

"Thank you, Mr Stone," the Captain said, clenching with pain. "Help me to sickbay."

"Why not? If we can make it before the ship disappears under us." I hoisted him up, getting his arm around my shoulders and lifting him off of the splintered wood that impaled him. It couldn't have been painless, but he didn't complain, so neither did I. "Will you tell me now Captain, why do you do all this?"

"Mr Stone," the Captain said, taking a deep rasping breath, teeth gritted with the pain even of speaking, "do you know what it is to lose everything? Wife, career, fortune, respect of colleagues?"

I clenched my jaw with exertion, and some sympathy. "Why do you think I do what I do? I cover up my own losses with my mercenary life."

As I assisted the Captain away from the bridge, pieces of the ship fell away at our feet as we dodged holes and falling debris. The underpinning of beams and buttresses, normally hidden behind planks and cladding, was visibly compromised. Now the animals were gone the ship was tearing itself to pieces, finishing the job as if with a will of its own. Nevertheless, I found adequate footing to allow us to cross the deck without further injury.

The ship was by now nearly abandoned. Although a few crew members remained, they were mostly concerned about their belongings or treasures.

"My powerful friends who owed me never repaid favours," the Captain continued. "They forsook me. My genius was scorned. My inventions credited to another."

"Well, now you're certainly on your own," I said.

"I don't expect you to understand me fully," he said. "Just allow me my revenge."

We crossed the obstacle course that the deck had become and arrived at the sick bay, or what was left of it. I interposed myself between it and the Captain, denying him entry.

"That I cannot do. If you're doing all this for revenge against society, then your mother didn't raise you very well, my Captain."

"How dare you," the Captain spat out. "What do you know about revenge? Not vengeance, but revenge! You're nothing but a glorified bounty hunter. Who are you to rebuke me?"

Emboldened by his words, the Captain appeared to forget his wound, though it still flowed with blood, as he launched a savage attack upon me.

I did my best, but I was no match for his oriental fighting style. My only chance was to try to pistol-whip him, but the moment I raised the butt of my gun against the Captain he disarmed me with admirable economy of movement, as if fighting were simply a way of relaxing and recuperating.

Behind him there was a cracked patch of floor, weakened, ready to give way.

I launched myself at him while attempting to take into account his peculiar method of deflecting my own momentum against me.

My strategy being to simply build up enough inertia, I caught him clumsily and brought him hard to the floor.

The damaged wood splintered under the weight of two grown men and gave below us, allowing us to drop with a sudden impact belowdecks.

Hurting and a little bit dazed, neither of us could get up before, still intertwined in our violent embrace, this floor collapsed below us as well. Dropping into the open air, we connected with the dusty desert ground with a thud.

Winded, we both stood up and assessed the situation. The broken and battered Sulinaut laboured along above us, erratic and deafening on its imbalanced wheels.

Maybe it was salvageable, or maybe it was going to rattle itself to death as it shuddered blindly on its way with nobody at the helm. Would it leave a trail of wreckage until there was nothing left of it?

The speculation was irrelevant. The ship was headed for a cliff edge, a sheer drop into the deep Coyote River Canyon. I could see the Captain's panic as he realised the danger to his beloved Sulinaut—if it went over the side it would certainly be lost to him, one loss too many in his blighted life.

Forgetting about me, the Captain ran for one of the ropes trailing underneath the ship, his only chance of saving the beleaguered vessel.

I gave chase. I couldn't risk the possibility, however small, that he might salvage some part of his ship and regroup, perhaps rebuilding the vessel and eventually continuing his murderous career. It had to stop.

I overtook the Captain and, in desperation, grabbed him by the coat. He turned and executed a kick which knocked me to the ground.

But I had delayed him at least enough to allow the Sulinaut to pass fully over us. Only a few ropes remained within reach, dragging along in the ship's wake, on which the Captain could still get a hold. He turned away from me and ran for one of them.

Painfully, I got up and sprinted after him.

Diving for it, he got hold of his line. While being dragged across the ground behind his ship, the Captain was slowly advancing, hand over hand, along the rope.

I exhausted myself with a final burst of speed, grabbing hold of the same rope as the Captain, a little behind him. I also climbed, pulling myself forward. Unlike the Captain, I only had to catch him, not the ship itself. Using every reserve of energy available to me, I gained on him by inches until I was in reach of his foot.

Looping the line around his boot, I held onto it, adding my own weight to the load he was pulling.

The injured Captain couldn't bear the additional burden, and lost his grip on the rope, though it was still twined around his boot. I let go, allowing him to be dragged behind the Sulinaut by his ankle, keel-hauled by his own ship.

The vessel shambled along, doing itself more and more damage, until it fell over the edge of the cliff, disappearing from my view.

I watched, anticipating my own satisfaction, as the Captain was dragged ever faster by the falling ship, clawing at the ground in a futile attempt to resist gravity and the massive juggernaut.

He neared the cliff edge. Near, nearer—nearer still—until...

Chapter 7 – Smoke Signals

The alarm clock—the harbinger of a new day, of rising and shining, of getting up and at 'em—rings its strident tones.

You hit the thing over the head, still failing to break it, only making the crack across its top a little longer.

You rise from your bed, grunting and swearing inwardly.

You go to your wardrobe and find a suit, shirt, and tie.

Minutes later, you're dressed and looking at yourself in the mirror.

The electronic bleeping of your black plastic cordless bedside phone startles you. You pick it up, reading the number in the caller display. "Good morning, Jessica."

"Hello Donovan. How long have you been up?"

"Wow," you say. "You're not even trying to pretend you aren't checking up on me. Your honesty is one of your best features."

"I could say the same about you."

"Okay, I'll play along. I've been up for a few minutes. Enthusiasm's hard to muster, but I'm managing it. Well, at least I'm making myself move."

"And you've got some prospects lined up for today?"

"I've got a newspaper, and there are a few interesting listings. Don't worry. I made a promise," you say, "and you're the only person I wouldn't dare disappoint."

"I'd expect nothing less. What are you having for breakfast?"

"By which I understand you to mean, 'have some breakfast'."

"Well, you ought to," she says commandingly. "Or at least a cup of coffee."

"I don't need one," you say with a hint of petulance.

"I know caffeine addiction has never been one of your weaknesses, but still…"

"I do feel kind of tired though. Of course, in the past, the prospect of hitting the streets in my ARV would be all the stimulus I needed. Maybe taking up coffee drinking wouldn't be such a bad idea."

"Have some, then," she says.

"Maybe."

"Hey, that's progress. At least there's no need to ask if you're dressed well."

"Neat. Tidy. Simple. It'll do. No one will give me a second look. Anonymity is the beauty of wearing a suit," you say, rolling your eyes and raising your brows as if she can see you. "The selection in my wardrobe is somewhat limited. I wouldn't hesitate to describe myself as boring."

"Well I wouldn't," she says.

"Wouldn't hesitate? Good. We agree then."

"I wouldn't," she says through clenched teeth, "describe you as boring."

"You're too kind."

"Okay. Last thing. Smile. Be cheerful. Win them over."

"Don't I always?"

"Hmm. No comment," she says. "Anyway, get busy. There's no time like the present."

"True. But it'll still be true tomorrow. Or next week."

"Donovan Stone!"

"All right. I'm going. See you later."

"Let me know how it went. Bye."

You replace the phone in its cradle.

Leaving your house and locking the door, you get into your car before consulting your newspaper to find out where you're going.

A glance at the employment section—it looks like you could do a lot of the things listed there—and a few cellphone calls later, and you're off. This should be a piece of cake.

First, a bank. You've seen the inside of these places often enough. You know what makes them tick. The manager agrees to see you. Fidgety, wishing he was somewhere else, he looks at a copy of your curriculum vitae. "I'm sorry Mr Stone, but you're under-qualified for this position," he says.

That didn't take long. If they're all as easy as this…

Second on your list, you try a factory on an industrial park. You've done some policing around here as well. This manager takes a little bit more time over your résumé. "You're very well qualified, but I'm afraid we just don't need you." He said a few other things too, but nothing you can remember. He was a boring guy—reminds you of yourself—and you wouldn't have wanted to work for him.

Marshalling some more mock enthusiasm, you continue the quest—your list isn't exhausted yet. Next stop, a security firm. This will be right up your street. "We could definitely use you, but there's not enough money to hire anyone right now." At least this guy seems honest.

After that the companies, premises, and managers seem to blend together, but the responses vary slightly, and you remember each one.

"The advertisement was a mistake. I'm sorry for wasting your time," says a supervisor, whose face and mannerisms etch themselves into your memory.

"I don't think you would fit our image," says a director, whose overall blandness you will never forget.

"Oh yeah, you're that cop I read about," says a consultant, who you would really like to forget.

Fed up with being undaunted, you decide you don't need this any more. You've fulfilled your obligation, and to spare.

Back in your car, you turn the key to start it up, and the radio comes on. The news. You might hear something about your former career, about your former colleagues, even possibly something about yourself.

But you never like the news, because it's usually bad. Death, destruction, murder, rape, robbery—sure, it was your work, but not because you liked those things. But you listen to it anyway.

The newsreader doles out the usual litany of depressing happenings which have little to do with you or anyone else. Putting on the news is a self-destructive tendency you share with most of the rest of humanity, of which you are a grudging member. But your thoughts wander to other things while the radio drones.

The newsreader's words begin to catch your attention. "—is down against the Yen seven and a half pence, and the pound has lost ten pence against the Euro, which is also taking a beating in currency markets. Today's run on the pound comes after the major losses on the FTSE, which closed at only—"

You turn off the radio, resisting the urge to break the knob off.

Putting the pedal down, you leave at speed—all you're lacking is a blue flashing light and the howling siren—with nary a moment to lose if you're to minimise the damage. You hope none of your former colleagues see you. It would be bad to attract their notice in the wrong way on only your first full day as a civilian.

You drive halfway across town as fast as you dare. It's too bad there aren't any bad guys to chase.

You reach your destination in record time, parking, entering the building, dashing up the stairs and into the office as if you were running down a perp.

The waiting area is full, presumably other clients who heard the same news as you. The receptionist in your broker's office is seated at her desk, doing some kind of paperwork.

She drops her pencil—almost throws it—on her papers and looks up at you with the world-weary glower that models so often assume in their photo shoots.

"Do you have an appointment?"

"I'd like to make one for right now," you say. "To see Mr Dallirama."

She looks back down at her paperwork. "The queue starts over there." She picks up her pencil and uses it to point into the crowded room.

You continue to stand over her until her patience breaks. Sure enough, she looks up at you. You keep her eye, willing the receptionist to break protocol and put you at the front of the queue.

Without taking her eyes off you, she opens the drawer, takes a pack of gum, removes one stick, unwraps it, puts it in her mouth, and begins chewing. She looks back down at her papers, brandishes her pencil, and continues her work.

Sighing and annoyed, nevertheless full of admiration for the receptionist and her coolness, you make your way to the end of the seated queue. You sit on the last of a row of folding chairs, out of place with the other more comfortable furniture that the customers at the top of the queue enjoy.

Aware of every second, half an hour later you have moved halfway up the queue, leaving the temporary chairs for the greater comfort of the sofa. Nobody else has joined the line after you, nor even entered the room, too close to closing time. You are the only suited client in the waiting room who has not loosened his tie, removed his coat, and rolled up his sleeves, though you slouch in your seat. You're also the only client who hasn't given in to the tattered magazines kindly provided by the firm.

"Next," the receptionist says, well past her quitting time and wishing she could go home.

One client gets up and enters the broker's office. Everyone to your right moves over one space. You wearily follow suit.

After another half hour, your will nearly broken, you are the only person in the queue.

"Next."

You rise, the stultifying wait having taken all the fight out of you, and enter the financial adviser's office.

Mr Dallirama, the broker who allegedly looks after your investments, is seated behind his expensive mahogany desk. Behind him and to his sides the books on his shelves form a vague impression of a spider's web, with Mr Dallirama in the centre. You have no trouble spotting the fake books on his shelf, behind which hides his safe. Hailing from India or Pakistan, he wears a much more expensive suit than you do, a Rolex watch complete with diamonds, and either a hair transplant or an expensive toupee atop his dark-skinned head.

He stands up to greet you. "Mr Stone, how do you do?" Mr Dallirama says in his accented voice. He holds his hand out for you to shake, but you don't acknowledge it. The very presence of the man brings the fight back into your blood.

"That's what I've come here to find out. Tell me about my investments," you demand.

"Very well. I'll make it quick and simple, since it's late."

"Good. There's no point drawing out the bad news."

Using a key tethered to his belt, the broker opens a file drawer under his desk from which he removes a folder with your name on it.

He lays your folder on his desk and opens it. After a few taps and swipes on his tablet, he has your financial life spread out before his eyes, for good or ill.

"In short, your portfolio is in bad shape." His accent makes him sound as if he doesn't care. The broker turns his tablet around to face you, showing a graph. Assuming it's meant to be read from left to right, it shows a steady upward trend for part of the way, and then a sharp downward inclination all the way to the baseline. The elegance and polish of the colourful graph almost makes financial ruin look attractive, but you understand the message well enough. "This crash has definitely taken its toll. Perhaps if you had opted to invest more conservatively…"

"You assured me that these were good investments," you say, standing up and stabbing your finger in his direction. "I acted on your advice."

"I also informed you of the risk," Mr Dallirama says, unmoved by your aggressive body language. "The decisions were yours. I can only analyze trends, I can't predict the future. I'm sorry, Mr Stone."

"You certainly are. A sorry excuse for a financial advisor." You take a few deep breaths, keeping yourself together. "All right, just consider my portfolio closed. If there's any money left in it at all I want it in cash as soon as possible," you say through clenched teeth, seeing red.

The broker puts his hand up as a gesture of caution. "That's really not advisable, Mr Stone. When the markets correct themselves—and they will—your holdings will adjust as well. Right now you still have those holdings. If you liquidate them then you'll have nothing. Just a little bit of cash, no potential for growth."

"So that's your advice, is it? Well," you say in the most measured tone your rage will allow, "I followed your advice before, and look where it got me. I want my money. Every penny."

You get up and briskly exit the room, hearing Mr Dallirama's exhausted exhalation as the door clicks shut.

The receptionist is still doing her paperwork, studiously ignoring you. "Next please," the tinny voice of the broker says through the intercom speaker. You'll be glad not to hear that voice again.

"He was the last for today," the receptionist says into the device.

"Thank goodness," Mr Dallirama says, as you try to slam the door, though its hydraulic dampener defeats your effort.

At least you still have your car, even if your finances are in a shambles. You sit down in the driver's seat and wait, hoping the trembling will die down as the redness recedes from the edges of your vision.

Did you do the right thing? Aren't investors usually supposed to hold on and ride out the storm? Wouldn't the markets have eventually readjusted, just as the man said? But now all you've got to show for it is pennies. From heaven.

Assuming heaven is responsible for your fortunes.

Too early to write the day off, you decide to visit Hudson again. Some nagging issues require discussion.

He's in the same room as you left him yesterday. As you arrive he's having his pulse taken by a male nurse, which is not his preference.

"Get out of here," he says to the young man. "I've got confidential matters to discuss with my friend."

"Friend?" you say.

"Hey," Hudson says as the nurse leaves, "it's nothing personal."

"Sure. How are they treating you?"

"It's a hospital," Hudson says. "They're trying to make me better, along with a thousand other patients. There just aren't enough pretty nurses to go around."

"I'll take that as an 'alright'." You get out your pad and pen. "I've been making some notes. I'm convinced the Madman supplied the weapons. There just aren't any other possibilities. There aren't many luxury arms dealers in this country, and he is local."

"Come on. You're forgetting our dear departed scallies. These guys were nobodies. They didn't have the resources."

"Unless they got the weapons on credit," you say. "They could've meant to use the proceeds from the bank job to pay for them."

"I think you got the wrong end of the stick," Hudson says. "They didn't rob that bank."

Your brain tries not to process this. "No? Then what were they doing there? Making a deposit?"

"We don't know. They opened fire on the street and got our attention. Then they took off to the Outlands. It was like some kind of trap."

"So they didn't make off with anything," you say.

"Not a scrap of scrip," he says. "In fact, none of them had any money of their own either. They were unemployed—unemployable even—and broke."

You rub your close-shaven chin. "They've got a benefactor bankrolling them."

"More like a malefactor," Hudson says. "A crazy rich guy?"

"A crazy homicidal maniac rich guy who gets his kicks committing murders vicariously. A string puller," you say as a misty memory plays in your mind. "He picked these men up from the streets, trained them, armed them, and gave them an outlet for their restlessness and aggression. Merciless killers at his command. Their lives are worth nothing to him, and they joyfully stood in front of our guns for the sake of an opportunity to kill. Their greatest thrill in life was to use the power he afforded them. He won't even be known by name to any of them."

"How are we gonna find him?" Hudson says. Chin rubbing is contagious, though his isn't as smooth. "Hmm. We could make some educated guesses here. He'd know how to cover his tracks, use laundered money for all his dirty business, leave no provable links between himself and the scallies. You know the deal."

"Yes," you say. "The deal that got one of us killed and put two more in hospital."

"Three. Severin's just a few doors down." Hudson pauses to gather some gravitas. "You saved my life that night, Don."

"It was nothing personal."

Less seriously, Hudson adds, "Although why you couldn't have taken a few bullets is a mystery to me."

"You know all that rubbish," you say disorientingly, "about their philanthropic causes and humanistic sympathies? It's a smokescreen. Those scallies had no values, not even the twisted ones of a terrorist."

"They certainly seem passionate about those causes, from the things they said in their letters and emails cribbed from their PCs."

"I'm telling you, it's a smokescreen." You pause, new thoughts dropping into your mind. "No. Smoke signals," you say, tapping a half-remembered memory. "Every time they mention 'liberating our oppressed brothers' or the like they're probably really talking about their weapon specifications, the time and date of their next meeting, or what they had for lunch."

"Come on Don, we're talking about common thugs here. Not trained wireless operators."

"Not by themselves, but remember their benefactor. He'll have made sure they were trained. If they weren't he could be caught or killed—and he wants them to do the dying, not him."

"Okay, maybe, but it's definitely not the same as other common codes we often see in the criminal community."

"Hot air."

"What?"

"Smoke signals. It's definitely coded. Pass it on and get the crypto boys onto it."

"Don, we don't have any 'crypto boys'."

"I know you've got some friends in army cryptography. Call in a favour."

"Ha! It's me who owes them favours. But I'll ask. And who shall I say this tip came from?"

"I don't mind if my name is mentioned."

"It won't be appreciated by a certain regal Superintendent."

"King Arthur can go… get himself impaled jousting. I'm not impressed by that pompous self-important dictator."

"That pomp—" Hudson began, "I mean, p-s-i-d—is my boss."

"Don't defend him."

"Who's defending him? I'm just not the type to put my job on the line by rubbishing my commanding officer. Maybe you could've learned that. But it's too late now."

"I got on for a long time without toadying up to him like you do, my flunky 'friend'."

"Hey Don, like I said, it's nothing personal."

"Absolutely," you say, turning your back on him. "Don't get well too soon."

Without consciously thinking about where you're going, you just start your engine and drive. You let the car take you where it will, like the city is a demented ouija board.

You only fool yourself that the car is leading you. You know where you're going.

In the evening twilight, when some men are arriving home to greet their wives and children, you arrive at Screwy Hughie's, your local pub. Your car takes a place in its generous car park, and you stop the engine. You used to come here sometimes with your colleagues, but it may be that nobody inside would even know you now.

The pub's sign is inviting and a warm glow emanates from the windows. You imagine the beer flowing from the taps, the clinking of the glasses, the steady murmur of conversation, some drunk getting riled and starting a fight. Anything's possible.

You anticipate the rich flavour of a stout, and the numbing effects of a few shots of Irish whiskey. A holiday to Ireland years ago gave you a taste for these things, and you've never forgotten it.

Who would it hurt if you numbed your mind in there? You don't even need to set an example any more. You're an unemployed civilian, with no obligations to anyone.

After anticipating the enticements inside the warm building for a least a full minute, you start your engine again and drive away.

You appreciate the colourful lights of the city as you pass under them on the busy streets. They look like they could electrocute you at any moment.

Arriving home in only a few long minutes, you exit the car and click the central locking control. Your front garden is bathed in a brief amber light as the car sets its alarm. You fumble with your keys, opening the front door and entering your house.

The cordless telephone you chucked across the room is still on the floor, conspicuous by its solitariness in the pathologically tidy living area. You pick it up.

The phone's display illuminates with the motion, and you look at it. No messages. A no-brainer. The phone has one purpose. One person to call.

The number is stored in the phone's memory, although you prefer to dial it manually, from your own memory. The rubbery buttons on the phone are small and hard to press with your trembling fingers, but after a few tries you succeed.

The call connects, the soft chirp signalling that her phone is ringing with her current favourite ringtone. Once. Twice. Three times.

"Hello?" Jessica's voice comes quietly through the handset.

"Jessica?"

"Donovan. I was just thinking about you," she says, her voice pleasant as ever. "What kind of day did you have?"

"Okay," you say, not exactly lying, just speaking before you think. "And you?"

"Fine," she says, "as usual. I've had a pretty useful day."

"Good," you say. "Is it too late to see you today?"

"Today? It's night time," she says. It's not dark yet, so your body clock hadn't taken that into account, but she's right. "And I'm kind of tired. It's been a busy day for me."

"How about tomorrow?"

"Why," Jessica says, "what's going on?"

"Please, I need to talk to you."

"Well, go ahead."

Your mind rebels. The plastic bundle of wires and circuit boards you're holding in your hand isn't good enough. "In person," you say, "not over the phone."

"Oh Donovan, you and your quirky ways. Everyone else uses the phone. Why can't you? All right, tomorrow afternoon, two o'clock. How's that?"

"All right," you say. "I'll see you tomorrow."

"Fine. I'll look forward to it. Now, you'd better get some sleep. You don't sound too good."

"I'm okay. Thanks. Bye." You press the hangup button and replace the phone on its charging cradle.

After being told you need sleep, you realise how tired you are.

You go through the motions of getting ready for, and into, bed.

It occurs to you that you have one investment that Mr Dallirama wasn't aware of. You sit up and grasp a vertical bar near the centre of your Edwardian-style brass headboard. It takes a bit of effort, but it comes away. Out of its centre drops a rolled up sheet of paper. You open it out, reading the printed details of the holdings it represents. Share certificates like this are rare nowadays, and this one is probably only good for antiquarian value, as the bottom of this company—like so many others—has surely dropped out today.

The document represents a memory from when life was good. You're as sentimental as the next guy.

Sure.

You drop the certificate on the floor, wedge the bar back into its place, and settle down to sleep.

But it's no good. Sleep won't come.

You wrench the bar out of its moorings again, recover the document, roll it up, insert it back into its metal camouflage, and jam it back into its place in the headboard. It's a tight fit and the metal whines with resistance.

You lie down again.

Soon, you are fast asleep.

The world has receded.

You are at peace.

Chapter 8 – The Treasure of Sirius Major

The town was otherworldly. The buildings, arcing upward in organic shapes because they were grown and not built; the vehicles, some of which floated on the yellow haze of a force field, and others which rolled on transparent wheels made of pure energy; the people, which ranged from aquatic creatures clothed in "spacesuits" containing the fluid they needed to breathe, to gasbag creatures that looked like biological hot air balloons with alien faces.

As well, the ships that docked in the port were otherworldly, some taking ridiculous and ungainly shapes, and others sticking to traditional graceful contours.

It was a dirty seedy place, both in terms of the dirt and grime that clung to everything, and in terms of the attitudes and morals of the lifeforms that populated it while their ships were refuelling and cargoes being transferred—much like profiteering spaceports on every planet.

All I'm trying to say is, there was nothing special about this place, except that I was stuck there, looking as dirty and seedy as the town, the grunge of spaceship exhaust sticking to me as it did to everyone and everything.

Milling through the crowd in my ragged clothes, looking for a mark, I spotted an unusual sight. Well-to-do homo sapiens. Who knew what they were doing here with their clean and tidy clothes, and clean and tidy manners.

No matter. I approached them, downcast, as pathetic as I knew how to look, avoiding eye contact. "Can you stake a fellow human for a meal?"

A man tossed me a twelve-froogil coin, a shiny silver disc with a bit of weight behind it, which I caught. It was a good thing that cash money was still in common use in places like this—panhandling would be a lot harder with ethermoney. I examined the little fortune and continued on my way.

I got a shave and a haircut at the only barbershop I knew that served humans. For an additional fee, they offered me a bath and laundry, which I accepted.

Then I went to the Swaying Grifflack, a favourite haunt, which served a decent meal at a decent price. I had taken a table near the bar and was eating my first hot meal in several days.

A rotund human in a white suit and Panama hat whose name was Ibonek, and a hideous tentacled creature dressed in black leather, were drinking and talking at the bar.

"—so the human says, 'I didn't know that about Arcturians.' Well, I had no choice—I had to disintegrate him didn't I?"

"I'd have done the same," Ibonek said, with a flourish.

"I'm glad you see it my way," Tentacle said. "So, have you hired all the hands for your freighter yet?"

"Yes, but since you shot one of them, I'll have to hire a replacement."

"Excuse me," I spoke up, "but I'm an experienced hand on a space freighter."

"Are you subject to space sickness when going aloft?" Ibonek asked, eyeing me suspiciously.

"No," I said.

"We take off tomorrow morning. Can you be at the spaceport by twenty seven hundred hours?"

"No problem."

"Bring your references."

The next day I reported for duty, with the prospect of getting away from this dive. The space freighter was huge, unwieldy, old, and unadorned. It looked more like a condemned building then a spacefaring vessel, okay as long as it kept space out and air in.

As I approached this hulk of a ship I was stopped at the gangplank by a female attendant with a face like a crustacean and a voice like honey. Based on her voice alone I was nearly tempted to marry outside my species. Or were there pheromones in the mix as well?

"May I see your references please?" the attendant said, her singsong tone threatening to melt me into a pool of compliant liquid at her feet. I focused instead on her face— antennae, eyes on stalks, sideways mandibles, red chitin instead of skin—it was an adequate antidote.

I clapped twice, activating my subcutaneous ethercloud implant, and opened my hands, suspending between them the holo-image which the attendant recorded and processed in milliseconds: my references, coupled with my biodata, medical records (doctored, of course) and various personal predilections I couldn't always hide from the device's event parser. "Looks good. Welcome aboard."

I moved up the gangplank and into the ship. It looked as rickety inside as out. But it made sense to trust the vessel with my safety. The cost of failing to keep a freighter space worthy were greater than those of keeping it in a minimum acceptable state of repair.

There was only one other human on board, a man named Erik, so I naturally gravitated to him.

For the next few weeks we were kept constantly busy on the ship's cargo run.

Erik and I were given only the most menial tasks to perform, humans being at the bottom of the galactic social ladder. Earth is located in the slums of the galaxy. Humans were from the ghetto, and few ever managed to rise above that. Our duties comprised swabbing the decks, peeling stellar-spuds, and occasionally going aloft to make basic repairs to antennas, dishes, and telemetry equipment outside the ship.

I had lied to Mr Ibonek. I was subject to space sickness. Only Erik knew. Returning from a spacewalk reduced to a quivering vegetable, I would be hidden in a cupboard until I came back to myself. I wasn't alone either. Several of the other crew members would similarly disappear for a while after a session outside the ship. It's a grotz eat grotz cosmos, and we did what we had to do to survive.

In a few long weeks we had made ten stops on ten planets, loading and unloading as many cargoes, and seeing very little other than the inside—and outside—of the ship.

There was a lot of money to be made in freight, especially with so many trading stops coordinated, but I didn't have a head for business. I would always be a manual worker.

Our contract ended on the same planet it began, in the same dirty bay at the same seedy spaceport. The same female alien attendant was at the bottom of the gangplank, processing the departing hired hands.

She updated the workers' references electronically, modifying their hand holograms with a virtual stylus. But she gave them their pay in cash, which was still a useful medium for exchange when you didn't want your activities traced. That applied as much to the freight company as it did to us.

Gradually, stuck at the end of the queue, we made our way down the ramp until it was our turn to be processed, patient but tired of waiting.

I was a little embarrassed. Erik and I looked worse than we did when we signed up, having neither shaved nor thoroughly washed for the entire journey.

The attendant still sounded like honey, and still exuded pheromones.

She told us to show her our data holograms, and went through the motions of updating our references. "Just a moment guys," she said. Looking in her cashbox, she frowned and spoke into her communicator. "Mr Ibonek, could you please come down here?"

"I'm already on my way," Ibonek said through the communicator.

I was suspicious. We had our references, but not our money. "There's not a problem, is there?"

"There might be," she said. "You can talk to Mr Ibonek about it."

Ibonek came down the gangplank, hands held up apologetically. "Gentlemen, we have a slight hold-up, I'm afraid."

"I hope it has nothing to do with our wages," I said.

"Nothing of the kind," Ibonek said. "It's just that we didn't withdraw enough cash today. A simple miscalculation. I can't pay you the full amount until I've had a chance to go to the bank. Will fifteen percent do for today?"

"I don't like it," I said.

"Me neither," Erik agreed.

"Please, just come to my office tomorrow for the remainder." He sounded so genuine and smiled in such a way that I wanted to give him the benefit of the doubt.

I eyed Ibonek warily, albeit in the light of the attendant's pheremones. "All right. What's the address of your office?"

Erik and I went our way, spending most of the token payment Ibonek gave us on a bed for the night in a flophouse. We were back to being broke.

So, as agreed, the next day we tried to look him up, finding ourselves standing in front of an alien blue movie house.

"3.1416 Andromeda Street. I don't think that's Ibonek's office," Erik said, eyeing up the decaying structure.

"That's what we get for trusting spacers," I added, before screwing the paper upon which the address was written into a ball and throwing it away.

After a couple nights sleeping rough, Erik and I got a handout and went back to the Swaying Grifflack for a drink of something other than water for the first time in days.

"Liter of Mercurian stout," I said.

"Same," Erik said.

The smell was pretty offensive. The purple scaled barkeeper listened to our order and accepted our money, while keeping as much distance from us as he could. I didn't blame him. I would have liked to put a lot of distance between me and myself.

The barkeeper gave us our drinks. We took them and wandered around, not wishing to impose our scents on anyone for very long.

At a corner table, his back to the room, I noticed a familiar humanoid hunched over a hearty meal. I nudged Erik, pointing at the man. "What have we here?"

Ibonek looked at us, unprepared. He must have forgotten this was where he first met me. "Ah, my dear gentlemen, how are you doing?"

"We went to your office the other day," I said, stepping up close to tower over him, "but you weren't there."

"Indeed. I seem to have been evicted in my absence," he said, all oily and evasive. "Let me tell you where my new office is."

"No need," I said. "You're here. We're here. Give us our money now."

"Quite impossible, my dear fellow," he said buoyantly, while sweat beaded on his brow. "I wouldn't dream of carrying that much money with me."

We were exasperated after three days of starvation and sleeping rough, without so much as the promise of being paid. As one, Erik and I pulled the startled and terrified Ibonek out of his chair.

We punched him, kicked him, and threw him to the floor unconscious, bloodied in his white suit. I found it more satisfying than I like to admit, then or now. I wasted no time in finding Ibonek's pocketbook and removing his cash, of which there was more than enough to pay the both of us.

The rest of the establishment's clientele continued with their drinks, avoiding looking at us. See no evil, receive no evil.

"Your cut," I said, counting out and handing a wad of cash to Erik.

I extracted my cut and a little extra in damages, and dropped the remainder on Ibonek's chest. "Your change," I said.

Ibonek stirred, groaning in pain, eyes still shut.

Erik and I made a quick exit.

In the evening, now shaved, clean, well fed (while avoiding the Swaying Grifflack), and clothed in something a bit better than rags, we found beds in a hostel dormitory.

It wasn't the Ritz, but nor was it a park bench. With a roof over our heads and coalpeat on the fire, it was the Ritz to us. We found a couple of human sized bunks and put down our stuff.

I lay down on my bunk and enjoyed the luxuriant softness, while ignoring the exposed foam, stains, and crusty bits.

Giving me no time to rest, a ragged old man—ragged, but human—approached us and introduced himself as Walt. He wore basic pants, patched, stitched, and held up by suspenders. His shirt was a cheap jersey, yellowed with spaceport grime. His boots were sturdy but holey, and he held a battered fedora in his hand.

In other words, he was dressed about the same as we were.

"Hey," Walt said, "are you guys privateers?"

"We ain't tourists," Erik said.

"I thought you was! I heard you talkin'. Don't get many humans round here. I got a proposition for you, then. I'm too old to follow this up on my own," Walt said, looking up and down the empty dormitory as he started patting himself down, looking for something in his pockets. "Ever heard of Sirius Major?"

I sat up, interested. "Who hasn't? Every spacer has dreams about the legendary treasure of Sirius Major."

"It ain't no legend," Walt revealed, a glimmer in his eye as he drew something out of his pocket. "I got the map to it right here."

Walt produced a small black box about the size of a matchbook. He pressed a button on the box, and it projected a flickering holographic star map in the air above it.

"I haven't seen one of those in decades," Erik said. "What a museum piece."

Yes, I was interested, but sceptical. Walt set the device down on the bed. The hologram wobbled a bit, rooted on the unsolid surface, as he put his hands in the image and manipulated it, zooming in on a planet labeled "Sirius Major." My mouth must have dropped open. This was a real star map, with constellations I recognised. This could be for real. My gut—or was it my avarice?—told me it was worth following up.

"I been figurin' it out," Walt said. "With a cheap ship for two million credits, and supplies for, say, five hundred grand, we could go and get that treasure. That is, if you're interested. I can put in half a million myself."

"Between the two of us we've probably got only five hundred grand," Erik said, "so we come up pretty short. Anyway, it doesn't matter. It's sure to be a hoax anyway."

"I'm telling you, it ain't no hoax," Walt said, on the defensive. "Well, maybe I can find us another partner or somethin'. Pity to have to split the treasure more'n three ways, though."

Even though we couldn't bankroll the expedition, we

weren't broke, so the three of us went for a meal together.

Now that we had been paid, we could afford some real food.

The golden arches of McDonald's—the next best food when you can't go to the Swaying Grifflack—greeted us with a banner in the window proclaiming their latest instant winner game with a grand prize of 1,500,000 credits.

We went to the counter to order lunch. The robots behind the counter were efficient. Erik and Walt were served first and went to find a table.

An elegant mechanoid in a posh McDonald's uniform brought me a tray containing a burger, fries, and a Coke.

"And here's your game card," the sleek uniformed android said. "Have a nice day." The 'bot floated away to serve its next customer.

I took my tray and moved through the cavernous restaurant, taking the anitgrav lift to the fortieth floor and the table where Erik and Walt were waiting for me.

Sitting down to my meal, I let Erik have my game card. "Here," I said. "I never win anything."

"Neither do I." Erik took it anyway and scratched the spot off. When he'd finished, a lavish colour holograph sprung up from the card, depicting animated stacks of money, cruise liners, jewellery, sunny beaches, and identity reassignment surgeries.

"Congratulations," came an electronic voice from the card. "You have just won one and a half million credits."

The card played a cheerful little tune, together with a pleasant but deafening klaxon that put all eyes upon us.

Reading one another's minds, Erik's eyes and mine met. Walt jumped out of his chair as if his youth had returned, and did a peculiar little victory dance.

"Just a minute," I said "how much of this is going to go on taxes? Probably most of it."

Erik's smile didn't dim. He leaned in close to me and said, "Ever since McDonald's declared its sovereignty it's been a tax haven. Your winnings are tax-free!" Erik whooped it up, joining Walt in his dance.

I kept my seat, still refusing to believe my good luck.

Later that same day, the three of us went to the used spacecraft dealer, going through the motions of haggling with the salesman.

The guy showed us to an overpriced spaceship.

"This heap looks like it's been through a supernova," Walt said to him, walking around the craft, kicking each of the support struts in turn.

"Hey, it's only got twenty thousand light years on the clock," the expensively dressed salesman replied. Six-armed suits were not cheap to make, and he had had his shell professionally shined very recently.

After the usual amount of this banter, haggling an inflated price against the shape of the ship, we had ourselves a spaceship—serviceable but at a modest price.

Our next stop was a local weapons and sporting goods warehouse. It only covered about two hundred square kilometres, while its car park accommodated fewer than two million vehicles. We couldn't expect any more. This was one of the lesser shopping planets. You would have to go to the galactic core to get the very best selection. But, of course, when we were walking around the shop or travelling from the clothing department to the cybernetics department by sub-supersonic lateral impellor, it still seemed like a pretty big place.

As with spacecraft, we stuck mainly to the second-hand sections. The salesman had shown us numerous weapons and prospecting gadgets, demonstrating them for us on the store's mining and shooting ranges. He was now lovingly caressing a large and imposing energy weapon. "This one was used in the galactic war of twenty-eight twelve. It's one of the most destructive weapons ever devised. We call it 'the battle axe'. Our people got to the battlefield as soon as the war ended, and collected around 60 million of these. Even pre-owned they've been selling like hotcakes. We've only got about two hundred thousand of them left, and they won't last the hour. It's a bargain at this price."

"We'll take it," we said. We could only afford one.

By the end of the day we were in our own landing bay, supervising the lifting of supplies onto our own ship. It was a joy to own a ship—to own anything, for that matter—let alone to be setting out on our own business adventure.

We were in no hurry to wait, having already spent too much time on this desiccated lump of a planet, so as soon as we were loaded up and cleared for takeoff we strapped ourselves in to our flight chairs.

The cockpit was grungy, but the instruments checked out. The ship was sound, in any case. We delayed only long enough to dust off the control banks.

"Three... two... one... here we go men," Erik said, relishing the countdown. The only one of us who'd done anything like this before was Walt, who was content to sit in the background and let us young folks do the work.

We felt the g-force as, through the windows of the cockpit, we saw the landscape drop away to be replaced with space and stars. I craned my neck to look down at the planet we were departing. The brightly coloured glowing signs pointing the way to the outlet stores flickered and enticed shoppers, projected from the nearest natural satellite— which was, of course, owned by the same people who owned the outlet mall. With any luck though, we would soon be shopping in the galactic core instead of slumming it here.

Our ship thundered into the unknown, the nameless planet we had departed receding fast—unless the planet was named Galaxy Four Outlet Stores: Great Shopping For Your Entire Family. In any case, our hopes and dreams were pinned to the ancient star map which hopefully wasn't mass produced by some local hustler.

After we had gone through all the motions of taking off and getting the ship on course there wasn't much else for us to do. The trip to Sirius Major would take about a year, taking into account hyperspace and wormholes, so we decided it was bedtime—unless any of us wanted to sit up and read a book instead.

In the sleeping quarters were six bunks, which was the maximum number of crew the ship could accommodate.

We chose the bunks that looked the cleanest and settled down to sleep. If there were any bedbugs, they'd be going to sleep as well.

As we lay down, transparent canopies were automatically drawn over our beds, which filled with a blue sleeping gas.

As soon as we were in deep sleep the ship's computer activated the sleep decelerators.

Within moments—so it seemed—an alarm sounded.

I opened my eyes to see the blue gas replaced with a red gas. I was almost instantly awake, feeling as though I had just had the best sleep of my life.

The canopies receded from our beds and the gas dissipated into the air, the air scrubbers quickly removing the red haze.

"There she is, boys," Walt said, looking through a small window at a grey planet. "The computer's woke us up just like he was supposed to. And there's our lady, at just the right co-ord's."

"Let's make planetfall then," I said. "I'm kind of anxious to get stinking rich."

"I second that," Erik said.

We scrambled out of our beds, hair, beards, and finger-nails long and in need of attention.

A little later, having made use of the ship's automatic barbering station, we entered the cockpit to see an offensive looking armed spaceship hovering conspicuously between us and the grey planet.

We sat down in our flight chairs and belted in, power-ing up our systems.

Erik shifted in his seat. "Who do you think is in there?"

"Looks like a pirate ship to me," Walt said, furrowing his brow. He operated a switch on his console. "You in the unidentified ship. Can we help you in some way?"

On our communications view screen an image appeared of a human, dark skinned, with a shock of long artificially grafted hair hanging unkempt over his own natural back and sides. He smiled an innocently guilty grin, showing a shiny gold tooth, and was oddly familiar to me, though I'd never had any direct experience with pirates.

"No, I'm Captain Dallirama from the, uhh... planetary security," the dishevelled captain said, putting a sombrero on his head. "We just want to know what's your business on planet Rine?"

"We—"

"Our reactor has a large leak," I said, cutting Walt off before he could tell the pirates any of the truth. "We need to set down on the planet immediately or we overheat. If you don't get out of our way and let us land our ship will explode and the resulting magnetic pulse will disable your life sup-port." I muted the communicator and leaned over to Erik. "Open our radiation shield for a moment. Their sensors will register a leak. Quick!"

"But the radiation—it may get us," Erik said.

"Would you rather risk possible damage or mutation from radiation, or the certainty that the pirates will board us, steal everything we have, and finish by killing us in some horrible way?"

"How long do I have to think about it?"

I grinned at him. "Not long."

Erik switched off the radiation shield while grinning back at me.

I switched the communicator back on. "So you won't hold us up, will you?"

"No, go ahead and land," the bandit captain said. "Get that thing fixed! Over and out."

"Thank you," I said. "You're too kind."

Putting the ne'er-do-wells out of our minds, Walt checked our holo-map, and we set down at the location indicated.

The lights dimmed and the hydraulics whined, fading until the only sound was the howling of the wind outside and the creaking of the ageing infrastructure inside.

Erik put a hand on my arm. "What's this that bandit said about 'planet Rine'? I thought this was Sirius Major."

"Rine is the local name for the largest planet in the Sirius system," I said. "Sirius Major."

We extended the gangplank and left the ship.

The landscape was grey as far as the eye could see. Everything—rocky spires and outcroppings, plants and trees—was bent in the wind's direction. I suspect the greyness of the plants and trees was not their natural colour, but simply dust saturation. Even the grey mountains in the distance were bent with the relentless wind. Not even the grey sky was immune, its clouds visibly representing the wind direction.

Our backs were laden with packs carrying high-tech prospecting equipment. The gale was strong, but not enough to carry us off our feet.

"Now, old man," I said, "I think it's time you told us exactly what we're looking for and how we find it. All I know is that the three dimensional X marks the spot on your map and that the X is at these coordinates."

"The treasure we're looking for is the plans for a device that will alter the structure of atoms and molecules and stuff so you can turn ordinary metals… or plastic or dirt or little fuzzy animals into gold or platinum or plutonium or little fuzzy animals."

"A matter transmuter?" I said, throwing my hands in the air in frustration. "Fat lot of good that does us. None of us have the technical know how to build it. So what do we do with these plans?"

"We sell 'em, you bonehead," Walt said, slapping my forehead with his palm. "We all get stinkin' rich!"

Erik smiled. "Oh man, that's beautiful. We get rich off this thing, and once somebody actually builds it the galactic economy collapses. I love it."

"Yeah, so do I," I agreed, appreciating the vision of it. Already the credit symbols danced before my eyes. "Just as long as we buy our designer planets before the economic meltdown. Next question. Where's it hidden?"

"Right here," Walt said, extending his arms sideways and spinning around. "We might be standing right next to it, but it's exactly three dimensions away. These gadgets we've brought will find the spot for us, and then drag it over into our three dimensions."

"Clever," I said. "It's buried in the gap between being and existing. Whoever buried it couldn't have guessed that in the future every hardware store would sell dimensional anomaly detectors."

Walt cut us off. "Okay boys, enough chatter. Start lookin'."

Each of us removed from our backpacks a wand device with a circular armature at the far end, connected by cables to the inscrutable electronic equipment on our backs.

Copout*Copout*

The three of us separated and began searching, waving our detectors slowly in front of ourselves, up and down and side to side.

After only a few minutes work, a whining sound emanated from Walt's detector. He took his hat off his head and waved it around while jumping up and down. "I've got something here!" he shouted.

Calming down, Walt took another cabled device from his pack. This one looked like a long, thick glass skewer with a rubberised handle. Holding the device, a dimensional extractor, next to the anomaly detector, its tip glowed as he activated it.

There was an electric flash in the air where the extractor touched something invisible, and an old boot materialised and dropped out of the air. Walt caught it and threw it hard to the ground. "Never mind, dadgummit, it's just junk."

Night fell. We went on searching, little encouraged.

We worked through the night, and day was breaking. Having found enough other bits of rubbish to stock a respectable junkyard, my detector now whined loudly. "I've found something big here."

I positioned my dimensional extractor and activated it, somewhat excited by the shower of sparks and energy arcs emanating from the air in front of the device.

After a number of blinding flashes, nothing had appeared, and the light show stopped.

"My extractor gadget won't bring it over," I said. "In fact it's stopped working."

Walt and Erik rushed over to join me, the dark circles of tiredness disappearing from under their eyes.

Walt looked at the equipment on my back, tapping a gauge dial with his knuckles. "It's out of juice."

Walt used his detector to find the same point, but when he used his extractor the result was the same. He couldn't

148

suppress a smile. "Well I'll be hornswaggled. Mine's gone too. This thing must be real big." Exhaling sharply, Walt threw his hands in the air in despair.

"Now don't get chicken hearted, old man," Erik said. "There's gotta be something we can do."

"We'll couple all three of the extractors to the atomic drive of our ship," I suggested. "That should be enough power to bring it across."

It took us a while, none of us being talented engineers, but by about midday we'd jerryrigged some cables from the ship. The cables extended to our backpacks, which now hummed with the overload. A hundred gigajoules of power on my back made me nervous, but danger to life and limb was part of any bold enterprise.

The three of us converged our extractor tips on the same point. I'm sure we all had the same thought—what if all this power just vaporises us?—but on the count of three we activated our extractors.

The air flashed and sizzled wildly, sparks showering from the point of convergence, heralding the breaching of the dimensions.

It wasn't long before a glowing black line appeared, infinitesimally thin, extending from the ground to a height of about six metres.

"All right! We've got one dimension of it," Walt shouted over the crackling of pure atomic energy. "Let's hope the equipment holds."

We were distracted from our work when, above the near-deafening rumble of our own equipment, we heard the thunder of a spaceship drive.

Surprised, we looked around for the source of the noise.

The same sinister ship we had seen while in orbit touched down nearby.

I grabbed a communicator off my belt.

"What do you want now?" I shouted without patience, holding the communicator in one hand while continuing to use my extractor with the other.

The distinctive accent of Captain Dallirama crackled from my communicator. "What are you guys doing now?"

"Welding," I said. "Repairing our ship like you told us to do. If you are planetary security, transmit us your identicodes in accordance with interstellar law, or leave us alone."

Captain Dallirama laughed. "Identicodes?" His laughing stopped abruptly. "We don't need no stinking identicodes!"

With a blinding flash of light, the line rising from the sand extended into a two-dimensional and partly transparent image of a stone mausoleum.

Walt, while continuing to hold his equipment, did his manic little victory dance again. "Only one more dimension to go!"

Captain Dallirama's ship opened up. He came out of it with his crew of cutthroats. We set our extractors down, locking the switches so that they would continue working unattended. Sparks continued to fly from the devices and their target.

"Stay here old man. Keep an eye on the equipment," I said.

I fingered the laser gun at my hip as Erik and I faced the bandits.

I spoke first. "What do you want from us?"

"There's a fine for landing here," Captain Dallirama said. "You better pay us or you might get some trouble."

"Or maybe you will," I said, drawing my gun and baring my teeth. "I don't believe you're planetary security. Who are you really?"

"We're freedom fighters!" The bandit spoke loudly with a crooked smile. His men laughed and shouted their support for his lies. "We support the oppressed people of the galaxy!"

"If that's true," I said, knowing it wasn't, "then you're on our side. We're oppressed. So get back in your ship and leave us alone."

"I was right, there's gonna be some trouble." Captain Dallirama and his crew turned their backs on us and walked back into their ship as if completely unthreatened.

Uneasily, I holstered my pistol as Erik and I turned, as if to go back to our work.

Within seconds laser beams cut into the air. A bolt took Erik in the arm. He yowled with pain.

We dove for cover behind some rocks. We really should have planned this a little more carefully.

I saw the pirates firing on us from the now open hatch. Some of them advanced toward us from the relative safety of their ship.

We fired on them but couldn't make any headway. Their cover was as good as ours, their weapons better, and their numbers greater.

Holding our own for a few minutes, we heard howling and barking. We looked around, as did the bandits, for the sound's source. It was getting louder.

Then, without further warning, they appeared. The Rinewolves, a huge pack of them running—practically stampeding—across the space between us and the bandits. Snarling, six-legged, doglike creatures, native to the planet Rine, they looked fierce but weren't given to attacking.

The way I saw it, we only had one way out of this that didn't involve surrender or early deaths.

There was no alternative. We needed the Battle Axe.

The bandits continued firing, even though they couldn't see us through the cloud of dust raised by the Rinewolves. I broke cover and ran for the ship, evading the random blasts that splintered the rocks behind me.

Inside the ship, I retrieved the weapon and took a

moment to acquaint myself with the controls. There was an intensity dial, a safety catch, and the trigger. How hard could it be?

The Wolves had passed and the dust was settling. From the cover of the ship, I levelled the weapon at our enemies and fired one round on minimum strength, aiming far enough away that whatever effect the weapon had would hopefully not touch us.

When the bolt found its target a small coruscating gravity bubble ruptured the spacetime continuum, drawing in everything within a ten metre radius. The pirates, their weapons, their ship, even the rocks and weeds, were sucked into the centre.

It was over in a moment.

All that was left was a tangled mass of metal, stone, plastic, and flesh.

Flung from the implosion, something landed at my feet. It was a leather pocketbook, apparently from the pocket of one of the bandits. It was seared and glowing along one edge. I picked it up, puzzling over it while walking back to our ship.

Respectfully, I put the Battle Axe back in its place before rejoining my friends.

"Looks like one of our freedom fighters lost his wallet."

Walt took it from me and inspected its contents. "Here, look at this." He handed me a list of names and comcodes.

"These guys were well-connected," I said. "What was their game?"

"These guys were two-bit banditos," Walt said. "They didn't know these people. Probably more of a wish-list."

More smokescreens. I threw the list over my shoulder and the wind carried it off.

While we were distracted with other things, the dimensional extractors had finished their work, and the stone mausoleum stood in three-dimensional solidity, encouraging us to enter and receive our prize.

We approached with an awe touching on reverence.

Entering cautiously, surrounded by darkness, a pedestal stood before us where a brilliant light shone upon an impressive parchment scroll.

Inscribed on the scroll were elegantly illuminated schematic diagrams, technical drawings decorated like an ancient religious manuscript.

I stepped forward and reached for the scroll.

The tingle in my fingers anticipated the touch of the treasure that would make me rich beyond my capacity to imagine. I extended my fingers to the pedestal, toward the scroll, extending my reach until my sinews ached...

Chapter 9 – Definitely Raging

The chimes of Big Ben peal through your head as if you were directly underneath the bells. Before they have finished, the echoing ringing recedes somewhat, replaced by the relentless pounding of a battering ram.

The sound fades. Moments elapse. Your modest Westminster-style electronic doorbell sounds its tones. An insistent knocking at the door follows the ringing of the bell.

Bleary eyed and disoriented, you get out of your bed and put on a dressing gown before staggering through the house—stumbling over the mess that isn't there—to the front door.

Hoping for a door-to-door salesman, you open it, ready to slam it again in somebody's face.

Instead you see two immaculately dressed and name-badged young men, sporting conservative haircuts. Each wears a rucksack and carries a religious book in his hand.

"Good morning sir," one of the men says, while the other just smiles at you. "We'd like to tell you about—"

You shut the door.

Wanting something to settle your rumbling gut, you go to the kitchen and open the cupboards. The larder is empty except for things you can't really eat, and so is the fridge. Breakfast was never your thing.

You decide to head for one of your favourite haunts.

Wearing your suit, your usual attire, you could be mistaken for a CID detective.

You look at your watch, the same one Melissa gave you on your last birthday together. It's later than you thought.

Tastefully arranged behind glass is a selection of doughnuts, cakes, and assorted sweet things. Icings, frostings, glazes, and sprinkles adorn the various confections.

Jimmie, ever friendly and patient, waits behind the counter for you to place your order, though he likely knows in advance what you're going to ask for. Jimmie's is the best bakery in the city, aimed specifically and squarely at those with a sweet tooth. Savouries are not on Jimmie's menu.

"Hi, Don," says Jimmie. Genuine sympathy exudes from his words. "I heard about what happened. I didn't really expect to see you here again." He looks over your shoulder at something or someone.

"Old habits die hard," you say, pointing at some of his tempting fare. "I'll have two of those, and one of these."

You hear the door open behind you, its cheerful little bell jingling. Out of reflex, you turn to see who or what is coming in.

You visibly deflate as Dave enters the shop. Failing to notice your reaction, he sees you and greets you with warm surprise. "Don! How's it going?"

"Now there's an intelligent question," you say.

"Yeah… well, anyway, I just wanted to tell you…"

"You already have."

Having put your money on the counter, you take your paper bag full of doughnuts.

"Well, just let me know if…"

You turn and exit the bakery, walking back along the quiet side street to where you parked your car, setting a brisk pace. Dave follows you at a run.

"Hold on a minute, Don," Dave snaps at you, trying but failing not to lose his patience. "Will you please talk to me for a minute? Is there some reason for the way you're acting toward me—and everyone else too?"

You open the dented car door and toss your bag of goodies onto the passenger seat. About to get in, you stop yourself, staring at the ground before you look Dave in the eye. You take a breath and say, "The reason is because I'm not—"

Dave holds up his hand to stop you, closing his eyes and shaking his head. "You should say, the reason is 'that', not 'because'."

You ball your fist and swing at Dave, catching him squarely on the jaw, hitting him pretty hard, but not as hard as you are able.

Dave stumbles backward, landing hard on his backside in the middle of the road, as you get into your car.

As you drive off, you can see him in your rearview mirror, rubbing his jaw and looking hurt—more his feelings than his face. Perhaps you should have hit him harder.

Forgetting your former friend—and by now he can no longer doubt the "former" part—you rummage in the paper bag and extract a doughnut, stuffing it in your mouth as you crank the wheel with one hand to round the corner. You have more important fish to fry.

"I mentioned your name, like you said," Hudson sat up in his bed. "King Arthur was none too happy. He said to keep your nose out of it. Leave the cops to do their work."

"I hope the cops will do their work. I'm just a civilian offering information and insight. It happens every day."

"Not in his world, it doesn't."

"I've been thinking some more about our poor dead scallies."

"Of course you have. Why else would you be here in this lovely hospital? Certainly not to spend the time of day."

"And one thing I'm sure, they weren't planetary security."

Hudson thinks for a moment about what you just said. "You're making me forget which one of us is on morphine."

"What did I say? Freedom fighters. Er, I mean, whatever they said they were—philanthropists or something."

"You mean all that stuff about Palestinians and Indian farmers? Sure. I think we've already established that they're full of—"

"Have you been looking at their chat transcripts?"

"No, not me personally. I am kind of stuck here you know. I think some of our guys have been looking for that, but chat rooms don't leave records on a PC."

"My guess is most of their communications will be via chatrooms," you say. "Probably rooms dedicated to film, and maybe antiques."

"Oh yeah? How do you know that?"

"Easy. The badges they wore on their balaclavas were Nirewolves."

"You've lost me again."

"Rinewolves," you stammer. "No. Wolverines."

"Oh, I get it. The X-Men."

"No. Red Dawn. The eighties film about a group of teenagers fending off the invading Russians on their own soil. It set a record at the time for the most acts of violence in a film."

"I didn't see that one," Hudson says.

"You call yourself a cop?"

"I just don't waste my time seeing every movie ever made like you do."

"Like I used to," you caution him. "Anyway, it's no wonder they liked it. And then there's the antique van."

"Yeah. Funny thing, that van."

"Oh?"

"It's not registered. It slipped through the net during the Second World War. It's got no aftermarket parts, and it's in great shape when it should be a mound of rust."

"You mean it was put in mothballs seventy years ago? I see. In that case, you might look at history chatrooms too," you say, holding him with your eyes. "Make no mistake.

The next bunch of these scallies is still out there. When you decode the dead ones' chats you can start looking for the second wave."

The seductive sound of Jessica's piano greets you as you stand on her grandma's doorstep, knocking on the front door.

The music stops. You hear the footfalls of her always buoyant pace.

After the locks are undone, the door opens and Jessica is there to greet you with a hug. She throws her arms around you, trilling with pleasure—the same pleasure she would afford her favourite brother or cousin.

She releases you, though you're ever so slightly slower to release her. "Donovan. You're early."

"Sorry. Would you like me to go away and come back in ten minutes?"

"Yeah. Or you could just wait out here on the doorstep."

"Tell you what," you say, "there's a pub down the road. I can fit in a few drinks in ten minutes…"

"Oh, I guess you'd better come in now. I can't have that on my conscience." Jessica holds the door wide open for you to enter.

"I don't know," you say, pointing your thumb over your shoulder, "I think I just talked myself into the pub."

"Donovan. Get in this house right now," Jessica says, swinging her arm to point inside with authority.

"Yes. Thanks. Your friendly persuasion is the best."

You enter and Jessica closes the door behind you.

"So, what's so important that you had to talk to me about?"

Nerves that never troubled you when engaged in a gunfight or handcuffing a violent offender rise up to bite your spine right now. You wring your hands and stare at the floor.

She puts her hand on your shoulder and guides you to the chair. "Sit down," she says calmly. "I'll get you something to drink. Chill down."

Keeping her eye on you, concerned, Jessica leaves the room.

You take a few deep breaths and rub your eyes, but you have little success relaxing.

Jessica comes back, holding a glass out to you, which you accept.

She sits opposite you, giving you her full attention. "Okay, Donovan Stone, what's going on inside that brain of yours?"

You take a few sips from your drink, and check your shoelaces. "We… we're getting closer," you say, looking at the glass and noting the etched designs. "To finding our perps."

"Oh," Jessica says with raised eyebrows. "I thought they were…"

"Dead? Well, I'm convinced there's another group out there. They did warn us, you know, about further demonstrations."

"And how are you doing this? Aren't you supposed to be looking for a new career?"

"It's not that easy. I can't just walk into another career. It takes time. And I can work this case as an informed private citizen."

"I guess so. I don't know much about these things. And I do know how hard it is for you, having to step away from the job you love. However, you did ask for it."

"Yes," you say with a breathy sigh. "I did. But don't be too sure I loved the job. The amount of stick I had to take from the high-ups despite the results I got drove me round the bend. At least I'm free of that now."

"Come on," Jessica says, "if you don't love it, why are you still doing it now? You're free of it, right?"

You look down, running your fingers along the patterns on the tumbler in your hand.

"Hudson—he's a colleague, and a sort of friend, I suppose—he's been working with me, but I think I've kind of alienated him. I never quite know the right thing to do or say. I'm not very good at keeping friends." You struggle in your mind to regain control over your words, which seem to be getting out anyway.

"Donovan," she says, eyes full of light, "I hope you don't think you're losing me. I'll always be your friend. I don't know why anybody wouldn't want to be your friend. You're great. Now, is that what was on your mind? Is that why you had to see me tonight?"

Okay. Just get your cards on the table. You take a deep breath. You drain the glass, failing to take notice of the taste or colour of its contents, and put it down on the coffee table, afraid that otherwise you would crush it and injure yourself.

"You asked me a couple days ago if I was dating anyone, remember? And I said I wasn't. Well, you know me better than anyone else does, and you've always been able to tell me what you're thinking, and you're pretty much the only one I can really talk to. I think I only haven't dated anyone else because I don't want to. We've been friends a long time, and, well… I think that… we already know each other so well, and I think that maybe it would work out if we got… closer. Do you think we could ever be more than… I mean, I feel more for you than just…" You pause, knowing how you want to finish the sentence, but the words won't come. You find yourself in an awkward silence.

While you've been speaking, Jessica has been patiently listening, but now she takes advantage of the silence.

"Donovan, you know I love you and value your friendship more than anything," she says slowly and carefully, "but if we ever were to be more than friends, I think it might be too easy for us to hurt each other, and I've always felt safe with you. We couldn't ever… Oh, Donovan, I don't know. I just don't know. How can I say this without hurting you? I know you understand what I mean. We're going to go our separate ways sometime. Aren't we?"

You endure an uneasy silence. Needing something to do with your hands, you pick up your glass from the table and examine your fingerprints.

"I hope you will always be my friend, Donovan."

An excellent question. Though not a question—as Dave would say—but a statement.

Of course you will. Could you even live without her?

"I shouldn't have said anything."

"Of course you should," she says. "We've always been honest with one another. I'm flattered that you think of me that way. I can't say I've never thought of it myself. It's just that…" She looks at you, and then at her knees.

Once again you set the empty, heavily fingerprinted, glass on the coffee table, as you rise from your seat.

"Never mind," you say. "You're probably right. I'll see you later."

You stand up and head for the door, and Jessica follows you. She may be concerned about how she has damaged you, but there's only one thing she could do to fix it, and she's not willing.

"Donovan, don't just leave. We're not done yet."

You grasp the door handle, twisting it, frustrated when it doesn't open. After undoing the lock, you try again, holding in check the desire to bypass the handle and just smash the door down. The door opens for you, filling your lungs with the cool night air.

She puts a hand on your arm to stop you, but you shake it off.

Casting an unintentional glance in Jessica's direction, you exit. Is it a trick of the light, or is there a tear on her face?

You might cry as well—if you were able.

Your blood begins to boil. You're no longer able to simply turn on your siren and part the traffic like a shark divides a school of fish.

There's a serious accident ahead. The police have made a cordon around it and brought the traffic to a standstill.

People are hurt, ambulance crews doing their jobs as the injured are dealt with, and you have nowhere special to be going.

You curse the idiot who had the gall to crash his car directly in your path. Nobody is moving, the disturbance being spread over the entire junction, leaving no route of escape for you or the other motorists.

You shut your engine off and do your best to settle in, resigning yourself to a long wait.

But your nerves are on edge, and inaction doesn't sit well. You need an outlet.

On that thought, as if by predestination, you see someone you recognise walking on the pavement.

Steve Gates.

And he's alone.

Getting out of your car and leaving it behind in the sprawl of stationary traffic, in a moment you are running after Gates.

Looking over his shoulder, he flees from you, seemingly startled and terrified. The chase is on.

His time spent inside doesn't help him here. Prison develops good bodybuilders, but not sprinters. You gain ground on him easily over the level ground.

Closer, but still out of your reach, Gates turns a corner behind a row of houses, getting himself out of your line of sight.

A second later, as you round the corner in pursuit, Gates, waiting in ambush, swings a discarded piece of wood at your shins, attempting to take your legs out from under you.

Prepared for that eventuality, you dive to the ground and roll, coming up on your feet.

You have what could almost be described as murder in your eyes, and you proceed to thrash Gates badly, wearing him down scientifically, using your feet or the flat of your hand to avoid drawing any of his blood or injuring yourself.

Bruising and—despite your best efforts—bloodying your enemy, you advance on him in a frenzy, having lost whatever cool you had.

But stupid luck comes to his rescue when you plant your foot on a wet and slimy flagstone, and stumble down to one knee.

Despite appearing to be beaten beyond recovery, Gates seizes the opportunity and kicks you hard across your face, changing the complexion of the fight—and your face—dramatically.

You sprawl backward and hit your head on the ground. Non-existent lights dance in front of your eyes, and then blackness takes you, just for a second, before the dancing lights reappear, superimposed over the swirling view of your surroundings.

Dazed but quickly recovering, and sporting a size nine bruise across your face, you see the blurry form of Gates running away through the fading colourful glamour over your eyes.

You try to rise, but can't. After taking a few more seconds to allow everything to settle down, you try again to rise, failing again.

The spinning world slows down still more. You stand.

Head hurting and dizzy, you walk painfully back the way you came as you adjust your tie, collar, and cuffs, ignoring the wet patches and smears of grime on your jacket and trousers.

Coming back in sight of the junction, you see it has been cleared of the traffic jam. Had you fallen unconscious after hitting your head? How long have you been away from your car?

Two police cruisers are parked near your car. One constable is noting down the details of the abandoned vehicle, while the other supervises the tow truck as it links up. You conceal yourself behind a parked van, watching the tow truck and the cops.

Spinning head notwithstanding, you have a long walk ahead of you.

Before long, through your slow gait and throbbing head, you hear your cellphone's standard squeaking ringtone that you could never be bothered to change. You fumble through your pockets, struggling to extract the device before it stops ringing and its messaging service kicks in. You fail.

You walk on for half a minute, and the wretched device starts ringing again. Once more, you go through the motions of getting it out, this time succeeding before it's too late.

"Stone," you say.

"Don. How's it going?"

You wonder why Hudson calls you by your first name. You've never done so with him.

"I have been better. And you? Oh yes, you're stuck in a hospital bed with a morphine drip."

"Yeah," Hudson says, "full of your usual good cheer, aren't you? But I'm not calling to exchange pleasantries with you—which, incidentally, I could do all day long."

"To what then," you say, "do I owe this extreme pleasure?"

"Hey Don, you don't sound too good. What's going on?"

"A tooth is giving me some trouble," you say as you probe a loosened tooth with your finger.

"Oh. Well, I thought you might be interested to know, our people found some leads. Some addresses and phone numbers in the dear departed perps' little black books and mobile phones, leading to some very interesting people."

"How interesting?"

"Very," Hudson says. "I'm not at liberty to divulge specifics, but there was an MP, a managing director of a very big company, a pro footballer, an American congressman, CEO of a bank, and quite a few others."

"You're right. It is interesting. I was convinced these guys were nobodies. And I still am. The facts of the case just don't favour this."

"Then that instinct of yours is still doing you proud. We—I mean my colleagues—contacted these people. They came away convinced that none of them knew our poor scallies, or had anything to do with the ambush in any way. These leads were just another smokescreen."

"Or a wish list," you say as you pick your steps carefully. "You're right. This is interesting. Thanks. Fat lot of good it does me, but thanks."

"One more thing. Our boys have been making some enquiries. They think they may actually have some leads on the elusive Madman. I can hardly believe it, but your ridiculous babblings might just be about to bear some fruit."

"Good. I just hope those ham-fisted CID boys can be subtle about their enquiries, and leave my name out of it."

"You're changing your tune. You said the other day that you didn't mind your name being mentioned."

"To King Arthur, sure. But not the Madman."

"You just have to have confidence in CID's discretion."

"You mean," you say, "as opposed to their indiscretions? Thanks for the tips."

You take the phone away from your ear and press the red hangup button.

The rain is beginning to wet your hair, and you still have a long walk ahead of you.

An hour of walking in the rain makes the inviting ambience of Screwy Hughie's that much more attractive—not only inviting, but essential.

No need to hesitate.

You push the front door and enter the pub. The only drinking establishment you've ever frequented, it's nevertheless unfamiliar. You haven't entered the place even once for nearly a year, and they've remodelled it inside and out—you remember seeing the scaffolding six months ago.

A live band plays Irish folk music, and the place is packed with people drinking and socialising. Not a single familiar face to be seen. Could all the staff and clientele have been replaced, along with the decor? But then it's crowded, and you can't see everyone.

You find a place at the bar and wait to be served—although it's not too late to leave if you want to maintain your good track record.

The barkeeper's Irish accent is also inviting. Funny, the previous barkeeper was Irish too. "Good evenin'. What'll you be drinkin'?"

"I don't know. It's been a while."

"I see," he said, his eyes penetrating deep into your core, as all the best barkeepers' eyes do. "Well, do you want to get really ragin' drunk, or just a bit drunk?"

"Raging," you say. "Definitely raging."

The barman looks you in the eyes for a moment, as if to evaluate the risk. Apparently satisfied, he grins a devious grin as he reaches below the bar to bring out a dusty and plainly unmarked brandy bottle.

"This stuff's not cheap by any standard, but it's what you're looking for."

The lingering cobwebs give the impression that the bottle was freshly plucked from mouldering pirates' treasure. The voodoo-in-a-bottle is attractive, though in a lucid moment you might wonder how a witch's brew such as this could attract you, designed as it was for the sole purpose of melting your brain cells and making you feel like a lawnmower was cutting the fur on your tongue.

But this is not one of those lucid moments.

"Give me two."

The barkeeper sets down two shot glasses and starts to fill one.

"I mean two bottles."

The barman suppresses a laugh—perhaps to be polite, or perhaps because he sees what's coming—spilling a small amount of the booze.

"In that case," he says in his Erin tones, "I'll definitely be requirin' payment in advance."

He gives you a second bottle, also unlabelled but a slightly different shape and colour. The barkeeper holds the bottle out to you, but as you attempt to take it from him you find he's reluctant to part with it. You play a game of tug-of-war with the bottle, afraid to grasp it too tightly for fear it will break.

You think you know the solution. You reach for your wallet and rummage through it, handing him a fifty pound note. Stand-off resolved, he releases the bottle to you.

The register beeps as he presses some buttons and the drawer opens. "Your change," the barkeeper says, giving you some coins. "I hope you know what you're doing," he says as he closes the cash till.

You look at your change disapprovingly, but don't count it before you drop it on the bar.

You take the lid off the mysterious bottle and fill a shot glass with the smoky liquid.

It tastes like fire. The effect is as if being whacked in the neck with an emerald shillelagh by a powerful leprechaun. You fear your eyes are about to pop out of your head and onto the bar, where they'll roll away never to see or be seen again.

Nevertheless, you fill both shot glasses, welcoming the pain.

Before you can screw up your courage to endure the torture and drink some more, a woman sits next to you in what you immediately fail to recognise as an obvious come-on.

You only glance at her for a moment, but you take in the full picture. She wears a skin-fitting top and short skirt which draw attention to her slender legs, full hips, slim waist, and ample cleavage. Made up only enough to highlight rather than decorate, her pouting lips are surmounted by a nose a model would pay extra for, with clear brown eyes defined by delicate cheekbones and elegant brows. Her silky brunette hair cascades down the feminine face to cover her smooth bare shoulders.

"Hi," she says, liltingly. "What's your name?" Her smooth tones are lightly accented, clear and easily understood rather than drowned in a regional drawl.

"Donovan," you say without a trace of emotion, looking down at the bar.

"I'm Sherrie."

"Hello." Still you don't look at her directly.

"Do you come here often?" she says. "I don't think I've ever seen you here before."

You sigh. "Yes, I come here often. But I usually don't get any further than the car park."

"But tonight you came in." A note of sympathetic concern creeps into her voice. If you would only look at her you'd probably see it in her face as well.

"I just want to stay out of sight," you say as you knock back one of the shots, feeling the Irish Inferno slide down your throat like sandpaper, "and out of my mind."

"You know, there are better ways to forget your troubles." She turns her bar stool to face you, shifting her body around in an effort to secure your attention. "Maybe I could suggest some of them to you."

Do you realise what she's offering you? She would go anywhere and do anything with you right now.

You look around the pub, taking an interest in the bottles behind the counter, the Irish memorabilia, the decor, and the band.

"Don't you," Sherrie said, leaning closer to speak softly in your ear, "find me attractive?"

You spare her another glance as she shifts her hips, crosses her legs, and subtly pushes her chest out. You look at your bottle, and at the dark brown liquid in your shot glass.

"No," you say.

You down another shot, and then refill both glasses.

The girl takes a breath but, though attempting to form them with her lips, can't seem to find words. She takes more breaths, erratically, raggedly, and suppresses a whimper. She backs off slowly before turning her back on you and walking away, her heels clattering noisily.

You turn to look at her now that she's leaving. She walks briskly, arms crossed, head down, leaving the pub, pushing the door open with her shoulder.

It looks like a few of her tears fell on the bar.

You turn back to your drink, grinning.

"You sure know how to handle a woman, pal," the barkeeper says.

You have no conception of the passage of time any more. Only of the passing of little glasses of potent Irish poison.

One of your bottles is dead, tipped on its side. The other bottle is halfway there.

Your vision is a confused whirl. The room is going somewhere without you. Is he stumbling, this man approaching you whose name you don't know? Or are your eyes and brains doing the stumbling? The unidentified man comes to stand over you, imposing his presence upon you. Even standing still, he sways and stumbles, though keeping a different rhythm to the rest of the room.

Not knowing his name, you assign him one. Joe. That way you'll be less likely to forget it, and if you do forget it you'll be less likely to offend him.

"Are you," Joe says, "Donovan Stone?" Joe leans in quite close to you, and his breath smells like yours must, a deeply aromatic fire from the depths of the pit.

You finish another shot and pour yourself one more, though by now your aim is so bad that you pour most of it on the bar, dousing your coins which still lie there.

"I've read all about you in the newspaper, Officer Stone. The maniac coward of Scotland Yard," Joe drawls, clearly finding words hard to come by, and swaying so badly that he threatens to bring you down with him.

You continue your drinking while Joe breathes down your neck.

"So Ossifer Stone," Joe says, "you're looking a bit 'stoned' tonight. Ha ha hah…"

You look at your watch, but you can't read it until you steady it with your other hand.

Joe laughs, writhing with mirth until he has no air left in his lungs, and even then he continues to laugh.

You turn and punch Joe, but not very well. Nevertheless, he takes a few steps backward, unsure whether to stay on his feet or submit to whatever alternative presents itself. Once your hands are free, the bar doesn't hold you up any more, and you stumble nearly to the point of letting the floor get the upper hand.

Before the floor can take any action against you, Joe, unhurt, takes a drunken swing at you, his fist appearing that much more massive when it's so near your face.

You feel no pain, so you assume he didn't hit you even though you reel.

Joe and you fight the fight of the inebriated.

Punches are exchanged, some connecting with empty air, others with empty heads.

"Hey Dave," the barkeeper shouts, "come over here!" Dave? You know that name, don't you?

Dave approaches you. He's wearing his street clothes. Yes, you know the name, and the face is familiar too.

Dave struggles with you and Joe, interposing himself between you, separating you from further violence. He easily subdues Joe, pushing him to the floor with a simple lunge.

"Don! You look terrible," Dave says, looking sympathetic and sorry for you. "What are you doing here?"

"Who are you?" you say, meaning every word. "Sorry. I—and a lot of other things—are out of my head."

"'Am.' Not 'are'. What's wrong with me? I'm correcting a drunk. I'm sorry Don, but I'm going to have to take you in and lock you up." Dave loops your arm around his shoulders, helping your unsteadiness.

"Great. Probably be the best thing that's happened to me all week." But you can't remember what has happened to you in the past week.

Dave shows his badge to Joe. "And you too mister. Come on."

Gently escorting you out of the bar, Dave is a bit rougher with Joe, taking him by the hand to help him to his feet, and then guiding him out of the place by the scruff of his neck.

Chapter 10 – In Hiding

Mud.

Everywhere, mud.

What was left of my platoon, depleted as it was, sheltered behind the crumbling shell of a building, the purpose of which could no longer be discerned. The village had been so badly hammered by bombs, mortar shells, and tank cannon that it looked as much like an archaeological dig as the remains of a working town.

The enemy had us more or less pinned down. We couldn't see them, but they were there, those same canon and mortars ready to fire at any sign of activity.

Sarge had broken cover for a split-second—attempting to save all our lives by finding us a safe path through the destruction—and they cut him down with a hail of bullets, leaving me in command of the platoon.

Even now the bullets rained down, chipping away at the brick and plaster that sheltered us. If it persisted, this most meagre cover would be worn away, leaving us exposed. Some kind of escape was necessary. We had already been informed that reinforcements could not be expected.

Our combat boots—our entire uniforms—were caked in mud and soaked by the never-ending rain. Lightning flashed and thunder cracked in the daytime gloom. Mud, rain, lightning, and thunder filled my memory, as if there had never been anything else.

I tried but could not remember anything except this war. No, not even the war—only this battle. Not the purpose, not the events leading up to it, not even how or when it began. This bombed out city and the lashing rain was my world, or at least the only part of the world that mattered.

I knew there were such things as warm hearths, comfortable armchairs, home and family... I certainly longed for them.

My wish list of comforts, extended to things like newspapers, sidewalk cafes, home cooked meals, a nine to five job, drives in the countryside, and glasses of iced water. None of it seemed like much to ask, except that it was impossible.

What good is a wish list if you can't use it? And I couldn't. The hot and cold of battle was all I had. I could wish until my brain turned blue, but war was life.

Over there, in the remains of a cobbled alley—where once there must have been commerce, flowers, street cafes, pretty girls, and excited children—might be a way through this hell of death and mud. I had been scoping out the area for a few minutes, and it seemed to be out of the line of fire, bordered on both sides with buildings offering good cover. It might be an escape route. But not for long. The buildings were nothing more than remnants, and they might collapse at any time.

I shouted some orders which were drowned out by gunfire, rockets, and thunder. We had heard nothing but the sounds of battle and weather for uncountable days. But Privates Dave and Arthur understood my gesture as I flicked my fingers toward the alley, consigning them to the jaws of the enemy.

I shouted and gestured to the other men, and the rest of us gave covering fire as Dave and Arthur ran across the open space making for the place I had indicated. The daytime darkness was immediately alight with a hellfire of machine guns and grenades. Before they could even get halfway across the street, still far from any cover, Arthur was killed and Dave was injured in the leg by enemy fire, his lifeblood draining fast.

Dave fell into a small crater left by a previous salvo of mortar fire, screaming for help. The crater gave him a modicum of cover, but they'd get him soon enough.

We couldn't just leave him there while he was still alive. I used the standard military sign language, sending Bert over to the crater to help Dave, without doubt sending him to his death.

The rest of us kept our guns blazing at an enemy we couldn't see—an enemy we hadn't seen since the battle began, however long ago that was.

Beyond any hope, Bert successfully reached Dave, and wasted no time in grabbing him by the scruff of the neck and dragging him toward the relative safety of the alley. Bert's determination, moving slowly in the line of fire, should have moved me, but failed. I had seen too many useless gestures of sacrifice.

We shouted for all we were worth at Bert, urging him on, encouraging him to hurry, knowing all the while that it was useless. He continued to drag Dave, giving no heed to the traces of death burning through the air all around him, which miraculously failed to connect with him so far.

Bert took a bullet in the chest, then an arm, then a leg, but he kept moving, grinding his teeth with agony as he defied death to get Dave to a place of safety.

The next few bullets hit Dave, finishing him off, and lightening the load as Dave's soul left him.

When Bert noticed that Dave was dead, enraged in spite of his wounds, he advanced on the enemy, randomly firing as he went. Who could know if he achieved anything in his random frenzy? The invisible enemy had so far been impervious, both to our sight and to our weapons.

Doomed from the start of his vain attempt, lacking any chance or hope, Bert took a few more bullets before getting hit in the head and falling down as lifeless as his companion.

A nearby explosion sent a hail of brick and stone fragments showering over us and a cloud of smoke spreading across the road, obscuring our view of the battlefield and providing a temporary cover if we were quick.

It was the best chance we'd been given all day, and I took it. I ordered out my remaining men.

More explosions rang out, visible only as flashes of brightness in the midst of the smoke. They ran to the alley but when the smoke had cleared, my heart sank. The cover of the buildings was gone: destroyed while hidden by the choking haze, and leaving my men unprotected.

Terrified, the men scrambled for whatever scant cover they could find. Hughie hid behind a big tree, Erik took cover behind a boulder, and Hudson hid in the shadow of an overturned truck. They all looked pretty safe to me.

I could see them all from my hiding place, having stayed put when I gave the order to move. Well, somebody had to keep an eye on the situation.

As one, the enemy concentrated their fire on Hughie's tree. It could offer little resistance to their combined fire and was torn to shreds in a matter of moments. When Hughie was left with no cover, they cut him down easily, leaving his wife a widow and his new baby whom he had never seen fatherless.

I didn't move. There was nothing I could have done.

Taking cover behind his seemingly impregnable boulder—the enemy were now chipping away at it, but it would take hours to wear it down completely—Erik fired sporadically at the enemies he could not see. Concentrating on trying to make some headway against them, Erik didn't notice a hand grenade which rolled gently and came to rest at his feet.

I opened my mouth, putting all my breath behind my voice to warn him, but no sound came—was it that my voice was paralysed, or that I couldn't shout loud enough to be heard?

Precious grim seconds passed while Erik, oblivious to the timed death at his feet, continued trying to penetrate the enemy's defence. The grenade detonated, spreading Erik around the battlefield as a fiery smear and a few charred pieces of flesh.

I clamped my eyes shut in despair. What did I do to help him? What could I have done?

Wrenching my eyes open again, I looked for Hudson—the last man making his futile last stand. I could see the relief on his face as the bullets impacting on the metal of the truck didn't penetrate, shielding him from that kind of death at least. A grenade landed next to him, ticking away the moments until doom, but at the last possible second he spotted it and threw it back before it exploded harmlessly in the air. Another chance to live, another chance—potentially, some time in the distant future—to be reunited with his family. Then Hudson looked terrified as he heard the distinctive zing of a rocket propelled grenade coming toward the truck, faster than the timed fuse of a grenade, and more inevitable. Gathering the power in his legs, he tried to spring away, but he was too late. The truck exploded, spreading burning petrol over Erik to finish the job the explosion had started.

I couldn't stand any more. I clamped my eyes shut. Had I been able, I might have gouged them out. My breath was coming hard and heavy. My entire platoon was gone, all hands lost while the enemy had suffered no losses that I could discern.

I could hear footsteps coming toward me from all directions, the inevitable march of combat boots, their owners converging on their last foe.

Closer... closer. They were upon me now, inescapable.

The footsteps stopped, just like my heart. The sounds of the battlefield froze, just like the feeling in my fingers and limbs—I couldn't feel the gun in my hand, the trigger under my finger.

Silence. It would have been welcome only a few minutes ago.

Even the lightning and rain stopped. The wind was replaced by a cold damp stillness.

I opened my eyes.

Enemy soldiers surrounded me, their faces obscured by helmets, masks, and bandanas, aiming their rifles at me at point blank range. They didn't appear to care if they might hit one another in the crossfire.

Their fingers were tightening, ever so slowly, on their triggers. They took their time, they drew it out, in no hurry.

At any instant, I expected the roar of gunfire, the peal of thunder...

Chapter 11 – Back Foot

Opening your eyes, which takes an effort, you see a white ceiling with a fluorescent strip light, flickering and in need of replacement. You're lying down on a cushioned ledge that does double duty as a bed and a seat—not immaculately clean, but it could be worse. An escape-proof grid in the wall to your side allows the offensive glare of the outside world to intrude into this place, whatever this place is.

Startled by your sudden realisation, you sit bolt upright.

Your mistake is apparent as your aching head throbs. Have you actually have been shot in the head by twenty masked soldiers?

Moving is bad, sitting up is worse. Eyes can't focus very well, and mouth tastes like sand mixed with lemon peels. Stomach pretty bad too.

"Hello," you shout, braving the consequences, "is anybody home?" The sharp ache upon speaking causes you to grip your hands with your head in an effort to right the world.

You don't have long to wait before a key rattles in the door. The metallic jingle seems much louder than it should, cutting a swathe through your brain via your eardrums.

The heavy and solid door creaks open like the portal to Dracula's castle. Two familiar men enter your cell, imposing themselves upon your solitude.

"Morning Don," Dave says, offering you a sandwich and a drink. Is it breakfast or lunch? And why would he be so nice to you anyway? "We were beginning to wonder if you'd ever wake up."

For just a moment you feel glad that Dave and Bert are alive. You wonder, just for a second, about Hudson and Hughie. But the feeling passes.

"Can one of you tell me what I'm doing here?" You never knew that hurting could make you speak so much.

"You got into a fight at Screwy Hughie's," Bert says, shrugging. "We had to arrest you."

"I did that? I guess that's something to be proud of," you say, with a modicum of shame. "Are you going to let me out of here?"

"Don't have to," Bert says. "It ain't locked."

Dave offers you the sandwich and drink again. "You should really eat something, Don."

Standing up, the ground sways beneath you. You open the cell door, gritting your teeth against the shrieking hinges.

"Do you want a lift home?" Dave adds. "You look like you could use it."

"No, I'll walk," you say. "I need to practice."

"Well can I have your sandwich?" Bert asks.

You stumble away, struggling to get your sea legs, holding on to things where you can.

You emerge from the police station into bright sunlight, bringing your eyes to the point of pain as you squint in an effort to resolve the details of your surroundings. The pedestrian crossing in front of you has a red signal which makes little impact upon your saturated retinas, and cars zoom by in the relentless mid-morning traffic—or is it afternoon traffic?

The artificial fluorescent lighting of the police station is no match for the sun's brightness. From its position in the sky you judge that it's still morning. Holding your hand like a visor over your eyes, you look both ways and proceed to cross the street. The squeal of rubber tyres startles you as a car smokes to stop mere inches from your legs.

Doggedly, you press on and reach the other side. You move through the locality you have patrolled a hundred times, and still get lost after turning a few too many corners.

You journey on through neighbourhoods which are familiar enough that you know you've been there before. But they're also so similar to one another that you might have been to their twins before. The instant transition from leafy urban terraces to squalid inner-city dumps and back again is evidence of your poor grasp on the passage of time.

Finding yourself in a park with a number of familiar features, you know you're not far from home, but you are having trouble working out which direction home is. This sort of brain work is tiring, especially with the accompanying aches of legs, head, and gut. You need a rest, so you take a seat on a nearby bench.

Elderly people push their grandchildren along in prams, lovers walk hand-in-hand, joggers jog, dogs run ahead of their masters, and mothers shout at their small children.

They're all normal people doing normal things.

You used to be involved with them—only on a professional basis of course. You took their statements, learned their stories, went into their houses, met them on the streets. Sometimes they wanted comfort from you, though you couldn't give it. Professional detachment.

The normal people would only allow you in so far. Not for you the friends, lovers, children of ordinary life.

A vaguely remembered wish list of such things surfaces through the fug that is your mind. Warm hearths, comfortable armchairs, home and family.

But what good is a wish list if you can't use it?

Right now you have responsibility for just one person, and you accept that responsibility and embrace it. You're going to look after number one. Your new motto.

The normal people, their children, and their dogs, are using this park as they will until the end of civilisation.

Everyone has someone.

Except for that woman.

She looks vaguely familiar with her well-turned appearance and expensive handbag. Her clothes are different—she's dressed for business in a smart suit, taking the place of her revealing evening attire. Geri? Mary? Cherry? It doesn't matter, she has nothing to do with you, nor will she ever. You don't remember exactly what you said, but you know you insulted her, badly.

Like you, she is alone.

Or is she? A hooded man in athletic clothes is running to catch up with her.

How do you know he wants to catch up with her? Couldn't he simply be a normal jogger? After years of walking the beat, of driving a squad car, of tracking down thieves and murderers, you just know.

Your instinct is all you've got left. And it tells you there is something not right about this jogger.

A moment ago you were lethargic and spent. Now, this guy has you coiled like a spring. You watch and wait to see what he'll do. You need evidence before... before what?

The jogger catches up to the woman, grabbing her handbag and knocking her down violently with his shoulder. Wrenching her arm, possibly dislocating it, the tough leather strap snaps, and he's off and running at an Olympic pace.

Why are you so coiled? That spring isn't you any more. Crime isn't your fight any more.

You try to relax, you try to look the other way. But you can't keep your eyes on any of the other people or scenery, as if a dazzling spotlight is shining down on the fleeing perpetrator, visible only to you.

Why me? you think. Why now? It's not my problem. I don't need it, and I don't want it. What was she doing carrying an expensive handbag around in the park anyway?

Sherrie is crouching, dazed and confused, on the ground with a bleeding elbow and a dislocated shoulder.

Before you realise you've moved, you're chasing after the jogger, grinning.

Pushing yourself to your limit, you close the distance between you and the jogger, his initial burst of speed exhausted. He's noticed you chasing him, and he gives his flight his best effort, but you catch him up and tangle your legs with his, bringing him down hard. You go down too, but roll and come up on your feet, aching but otherwise unhurt. Young and fit, the jogger is quickly back on his feet as well.

About to grab the handbag from him, you stop as you notice a big wild-looking man standing nearby, a sadistic grin chiseled into his face.

You look around. You've been led, almost herded, into a clearing in the trees and shrubs. There's no line of sight to any other public areas, nor to any people who could act as witnesses.

The jogger circles behind you, boxing you in.

"Our information about you is pretty accurate, Inspector," the large man said, his eyes wide. "It was too easy to lead you to this secluded beauty spot."

One guy behind, and one in front. Yes, the one in front is big, but the bigger they are—

You strike behind yourself with your leg, plunging your foot into the jogger's gut as his lungs audibly deflate.

Now on your back foot, you swing your fist as hard as your posture allows into the big man's face. He stumbles backward a step or two.

The big man recovers fast, resuming his stance, his mouth bleeding. "Whoa!" he shouts. "Do that again! Makes me feel alive!" He speaks with a gleeful smile and murderous eyes. About six feet five inches, he's muscled as well as having a beer gut. His hair is wild and hangs down to his shoulders. Wearing a dark suit, sans tie, and a badge on the lapel carrying the slogan, "I hate cops", he's just asking to be taken into custody.

"The Madman, I presume," you say.

"At your punching-bag service. Now, enough with the small talk. You've been making enquiries. You wanted to meet me."

"You're making a mistake," you say. "I'm not a cop anymore. The police don't even want to know what I have to say."

"You misunderestimate yourself. Your name wasn't mentioned. At least not right away. A guy like me has gotta know how to read between the lines."

"Consider me informed," you say. "Now, you can consider yourself under arrest. Citizen's arrest."

"Well, Mr Stone, I'm not coming without a fight. You know that, don't you? Of course you do. See, I've got a different perspective on this meeting. When a cop gets to meet me, only one of us can go back into civilization to pick up where we left off in our favourite video games. I don't know about you, but I haven't had to abandon a game yet, and I'm determined to find out how Call of Duty ends."

How he can be so confident in his threat, when his crony is still writhing on the ground clutching his gut, you can't tell. "I assume you have some way to odd the evens. Show me right now, or you might as well just start marching to the station."

"Come on, Mr Stone. I'll be a lot harder to beat than my little slave there. He's just a guy I paid to do a simple job. A contractor. Now," the Madman says, almost drooling, "hit me again."

"Your leverage," you bite out. "Now!"

"Okay, fine. I just wanted to have a little fun with you first, but never mind." The Madman whistles shrilly.

Another tough looking goon shuffles out from behind a tree. (You recognise this one—it's Stephen Gates.) He escorts a gagged Jessica, to whose neck he holds a knife.

Your vision goes blurry, and your heart races. Light-headed and giddy your legs threaten to fold. You forget to breathe for a desensitised moment, then take deep breaths, getting the oxygen flowing and marshalling your strength.

"What exactly do you expect me to do?"

The Madman smiles more murder at you. "You are going to lay down your life for your friend. After hitting me a few more times, of course. But you are not going to make any effort to save her from me, or else she'll be killed instantly."

You continue to breathe deeply. You need enough oxygen to relieve the pain, and to make it possible to speak.

"Are you mad? Stupid question, I know. I don't believe for a second you won't kill her as soon as you're done with me."

In Jessica's eyes you see terror. But there's something else too.

"Unless we can come to some kind of better arrangement," you say, "then it's not going to happen your way."

"Don't worry, Mr Stone. I've thought of that. That's why I've called the press."

Another whistle.

Another figure steps into the scene from behind a tree. Lawrence Murphy. He holds an expensive and chunky digital SLR camera. Your heart sinks.

"Your good friend Mr Murphy will officiate, armed with nothing more than a pen and a camera, to keep me… honest." The word slimes from his mouth.

The Madman might be able to convince you after all. Murphy is certainly spineless enough to do the job.

"We've come to an understanding," Murphy says. "I get an exclusive, and the girl gets out safely. Everyone wins. Except you."

Your head spins while trying to work out the details of this scenario. Could it work? Could Murphy oil his way out of an aiding and abetting charge on account of the implied threat to his own life? Or was the Madman so mad he thought this crazy plan would come to something? Who knows what Murphy is thinking, but you're sure the Madman will not leave here without making sure there are three bodies, maybe four, for Joe Public to discover.

Murphy circles the scene, his camera clicking as he takes photos. You look at his face and see sweat streaming down. It's not that warm. You wonder if he has nerves after all. He certainly has some nerve.

"Okay," you say to the Madman, "you win. But I get to hit you a few times first, right?"

He nods. "Yes. Well... twice. But I might hit back. And I'm bigger than you."

"Fair enough." You look at Gates. "Remember, he wants me to hit him. So you stay calm."

You sneak a look at Jessica. Her eyes meet yours.

The thing you see in her eyes, apart from terror, is trust.

You step closer to the Madman, as Murphy continues circling and taking pictures.

You ball your fist and pull it back.

Murphy, behind Gates, goes for an over-the-shoulder shot, for which you are striking an arresting pose.

Gates's eyes are glued to you and the Madman.

You strike, pulling your right hook somewhat, taking him full on the jaw.

He staggers back a little. Touching his jaw and finding no blood there, he says, "I know you can do better than that." His eyes are disappointed. He's begging for pain.

You give it to him.

You raise your fist again, but while his eye is on your fist, you lash out with your hardest, fastest side kick, taking him in the abdomen. You hear a rib snap as he staggers back to fall into a sitting position.

The Madman is fighting for breath. "Not fair," he croaks, "but I like it." His teeth are bared with pain and the hint of a smile.

He stands up. Murphy remains approximately behind Gates.

"Now it's my turn," the Madman says. He brandishes his large fist, but is distracted by a loud smashing sound.

Bits of Murphy's camera—lenses, metal rings, and plastic shards—fall to the ground, except for a few pieces which are embedded in Gates's skull.

You grab the Madman's raised fist and, drawing him close to you, break his crooked nose with your forehead.

The terrified Murphy runs, disappearing from the clearing.

You smash your aching fist into the Madman's nose, pulping it as you attempt to bring him to a threshold of pain that he will not enjoy.

Jessica, tears streaming from her face, is watching, helpless. Gates, on all fours, is recovering from the expensive blow to his head.

"Run!" you shout to her, as you aim another blow at the Madman's face. He drops to his knees.

Jessica looks around for something.

"Get out of here—get help!" You kick the Madman in the gut again, before kneeing him in the face. By now his nose is a flattened mess, but he's still very conscious.

Jessica has raised a stone over the kneeling Gates's head, and brings it down hard, her eyes streaming with tears. It's clear that she isn't leaving.

"Him too," you say, pointing at the jogger, who has been watching until now.

Jessica, with her stone still in her hands, looks at the poor hireling. He gets up and runs away.

"Okay," you say to the Madman, "it's just the three of us now. You know who I'm looking for. The scum you've been selling weapons to. The second wave of those humanitarian suicide crazies. Who are they, and where do I find them?"

"I know who you mean," he says, sounding as if he has a severe cold. Blood spatters from the remains of his nose as he speaks. "The nobodies. The trained monkeys. I didn't sell 'em weapons. I gave 'em weapons. For free."

"You are the benefactor? Why? There's no money in it."

He laughs. Not a pretty sight. You think you see a chip of bone fly from his nasal area. "Oh, they had their shopping list of potential benefactors, but none of them understood what was being asked of them. Or they weren't interested. Me, I've got plenty of money already. But these young morons' had such pure desire. Simple. They love the guns. Profound. They so want to use 'em. Lovely. They just needed a chance. Someone to believe in 'em."

With your foot you break another of his ribs. "Who are they? What are their addresses? Phone numbers?"

"Ooh," he moans. "That hurts… so good."

You get in close and punch him across the jaw once more.

Something in his hand glints like a mirror in the sun as he moves it fast.

Once isn't enough, and you bring your other fist down on him.

"I don't keep that kind of info in my head. And if I did," he says with waning strength, "it kind of hurts right now."

You look down at his hand. Whatever glinted is gone, but his hand is covered in blood.

A couple more swings at his scarcely recognisable face, and you are swooning giddily. Too much adrenaline, or something.

"Tell me," you command, swaying with tiredness, "now."

The Madman responds with a sickly laugh.

A stone comes down on the Madman's head. He crumples to the soily ground.

Jessica drops the stone with a squelchy thud. "He wasn't going to tell you anything." Her eyes are red with tears. "And you need help." She points at your midsection.

"And you have helped me," you say. "Thanks." You look around. "Now to return this to its rightful owner." You pick up the handbag, the thing that drew you to this clearing.

Looking at the prize you have won, the formerly expensive handbag—now torn and worthless—still intact with whatever contents it carries, you turn to head back to Sherrie.

Jessica takes your arm, steadying you. "Donovan, that's not important right now."

As you exit the clearing you see Sherrie, walking in your direction.

Clutching her damaged shoulder with her good hand, she looks concerned as she makes her way toward you. You hold her handbag up for her to see, hoping it was worth the trouble. If it's not full of credit cards, cash, and expensive jewellery you'll be very disappointed.

You hand the bag over to her. She takes it from you but doesn't seem interested in receiving it, instead examining you from head to toe with horror. Ignoring her, you realise how tired you are, and turn away to make another attempt at finding your way home. It may be difficult, because you feel that the effect of the alcohol is returning, bringing disorientation with it.

"Mr Stone?" Sherrie says, sounding as if she is a million miles away, and looking very concerned in her disorientating way.

"Donovan, come and sit down," Jessica says, still at your elbow and pointing to a nearby bench.

What was a moment ago only a cold feeling in your gut now expands to include pain and nausea. You put your hand down there instinctively, and it feels wet and warm. So where is the chill coming from?

Red. Your hand is completely red.

Your vision is fuzzy as you look down at your abdomen. A soaking red stain spreads out from a jagged gash in your shirt.

Why did you never stop to think the Madman might have a weapon?

The world spins around you, accompanied by coloured lights and shooting stars that dance across your vision. You sway and stumble like a drunk.

You collapse to the ground none too gently. Suddenly, all those people you watched with such envy doing their own thing and having a good time on the park are standing around you, mixing concern and fascination.

"Look at all that blood," says one of the bystanders. "He'll never make it."

Jessica is kneeling at your side, wetting your jacket with her tears. "Donovan," she sobs. "Donovan!"

The last thing you hear is an ambulance siren, lulling you gently to sleep with its banshee wail.

The blackness takes you, and you welcome it.

Chapter 12 – Agent Provocateur

The mountain, lined with ice, was capped with snow, which was in turn topped by a fortress-like building.

The equipment on my belt and in my backpack clinked and rattled, as I lifted my ice axe and swung it hard to gain purchase in the ice above me. Trusting most of my weight to the two axes in my gloved hands, I brought my feet up to secure the crampons' spikes in the ice, allowing me to straighten my legs and gain a half-metre of altitude.

Breaking the silence of the mountain, an alarm began wailing at the top.

Voices shouting and conferring with one another.

Then, automatic weapon fire.

Chunks of ice flew all around me, as dangerous as the bullets. I quickly looked everywhere for a means of escape.

The gunfire chipped away the ice around my axes, releasing their anchorage. I slid away rapidly.

After falling a few metres I caught myself by catching a rough rocky outcrop with an axe.

I pressed myself down as tightly as I could underneath the rock, a suitable refuge from flying bullets.

I reached into my backpack with my free hand for a pair of dark goggles to protect my eyes, both from the sun and from shrapnel. I also extracted my compact submachine gun.

With only one hand free, I held the gun's shoulder strap in my teeth before extracting an ammo clip from my backpack. The free ice axe swung wildly on its leash.

I loaded the weapon one-handed and looped the strap around my neck.

Emerging from my cover, I fired. My first bullets hit the wall from behind which the guard was firing. I raised my aim a little bit and took him down.

I let the gun dangle from my neck, and climbed like a madman toward the outer wall of the fortress.

Two more guards fired at me.

Increasing my pace, I made a sideways leap for shelter under some more rocks. A bullet sparked off one of my axes.

The axe flew from my hand, leaving me anchored by the one remaining.

I dug my crampon into the ice and resumed climbing with only one axe, heading for the opposite side of my rocky cover while flattening down low.

Showing as little of myself as possible, I emerged from cover as they were still keeping their eyes on the spot where I had disappeared from their view. I shot at the two guards, killing them both.

I quickly climbed up to the wall as the last swing of my ice axe left it firmly embedded. I had to leave it as I got a hand, then my head, over the top, finally hefting myself up and over.

I collected what I needed from the selection of weapons available to me on and around the bodies, and ran cautiously but quickly into the compound.

I rounded a corner and was confronted with a very large window, behind which was a luxuriously furnished room, an impressive refuge from the snow and cold.

There were several people behind the window, the men in tuxedos and the ladies in evening dresses, seemingly holding a genteel cocktail party.

The people noticed me and came to the window, watching me with interest.

I pointed my weapon at them, but they only smiled, waved, and sipped their drinks. I fired at the window, emptying the clip of ammunition, and it didn't break.

The clip was empty. I replaced it with a fresh one. Now the people inside were laughing at me.

Removing a grenade from the pouch on my belt and holding it up for them to see, they stopped laughing. I pulled the pin and set the grenade down near the window. They now moved in a frenzy, looking for cover. I waved at them, smiling, and moved around the corner.

I heard the explosion and reemerged into smoke and confusion.

The window was gone. Some of the people were lacerated from the shattered glass. All surrendered to me.

Covering them with my submachine gun, I was about to take my goggles off, when someone, a woman whose face I couldn't see, made a dash for a door at the back of the room.

She was fast. I brought my weapon to bear on her and fired, but she made it out the door unscathed.

There was a large storage cupboard in the opposite corner. With a few warning shots over their heads, I herded my captives inside.

They entered the cupboard, and I barricaded it as best I could with a splintered antique sideboard.

Following the escapee through the back door, I found myself in a utilitarian room stocked with sports equipment—skis, boots, snowboards, winter clothes, one hang glider—and a large bay door standing open over the snow-covered mountainside.

The woman was fastening herself into the hang glider—but when I entered the room she paused to shoot at me. As I sidestepped for cover behind a rack of snowboards I got a good look at her face.

Jessica, my target for this mission.

I ran to her other side and flanked her, attempting to wrest the gun from her grip.

She was a better fighter than her somewhat incomplete dossier had suggested. With a twist of her wrist she quickly and effortlessly had me on the floor, winded and in pain, without leaving her position under the glider. Before I could get my breath back, she had completed her harness, launching the hang glider and herself into the open air.

I stood up painfully and grabbed a snowboard.

It was a long way down. I jumped out of the bay door and dropped some six metres before my feet and the board connected with the steep snow.

I looked to the skies, spotting the hang glider and giving chase.

The snow was wet and slick. What I lacked in control I made up for in speed.

Soaring out of my reach, Jessica flew over a rocky cliff. I was about to do the same, only without the benefit of wings.

I leaned back on the board, digging the edge into the snow, trying to stop.

The snowboard and I both tumbled.

The board sailed ahead of me over the edge of the cliff.

Digging my feet and fingers in, I came to a halt at the edge, headfirst. I looked down to see the snowboard dropping, until it clattered against some rocks a hundred meters down.

The hang glider, however, floated away. Profoundly tired and deflated, I lay in the snow until I recovered.

A few days later, back at headquarters in London, rested and mostly healed, I reported for briefing.

My commanding officer's receptionist, the dowdy but beautiful Sherrie, kept her desk in a proper civil service tidiness. Through her office window she had a commanding view of London—the Houses of Parliament, the Eye, the Tower, St Paul's, Tower Bridge. Impossibly, the whole city was visible from here.

"Good morning, Donovan. We've all missed you around here. Well, I have anyway. N is in a state today, and I think it's something to do with you," she said with a slight sneer. "Just what have you done this time?"

I moved close to her, perching on the edge of her desk. "Sherrie, I can't lie to you," I said, leaning down to bring my face nearer to hers. "I bungled a job. I was thinking of you, and I couldn't concentrate." I drew nearer still, and our lips were almost touching.

"I want to believe you, Donovan. Really I do." She inclined her head toward N's door. "Go on in."

Smiling back at Sherrie, I went through the door which was elegantly soundproofed with leather padding.

N's office was appointed with antique furniture and classic regency decor.

Middle-aged, balding, and dressed in a vintage Savile Row suit, N sat at his desk.

"Sit down, Number Seven," N said. "Now, tell us what went wrong."

"She got the upper hand, sir. It happens sometimes," I said. "Also, her boyfriend wasn't there as we had expected him to be."

"Never mind, Number Seven," N said. "We're going to try a different approach. It'll rely heavily on your renowned influence over the fair sex. You'll present yourself to her in a, shall we say, less violent manner, such that she'll betray her 'boyfriend' to you."

"You want me to make her fall in love with me?"

"Couldn't have said it better myself."

"Then maybe now you'll tell me exactly why we want him, sir?"

"Yes, of course," N said as he opened the file on his desk. "He's stolen a new weapon from McGuffin Electronics."

He handed me an artist's conception, together with a technical drawing.

N explained. "That's the McGuffin weapon. It's equipped with a revolutionary power cell which alone should be worth a king's ransom on the black market. Very high energy in a tiny package, and as yet only a prototype. Same for the McGuffin itself. Plasma beam I think is how they described it. Very destructive. The Company want them back as they stand to lose revenues if the thing is sold to their competitors, and they naturally will only trust us with the job. We're doing it because we don't want it in the hands of our competitors. Now listen to me Number Seven, if you bring this off, I personally guarantee you a promotion. And one other thing. The Company are offering a substantial cash reward to you if you can bring it back, working or not."

"Do you mean me or the McGuffin?" I quipped.

N pretended to smile, unconvincingly. "Take the job seriously, Number Seven." He ended the briefing.

I went down to the armoury, where I found the armourer tinkering with something electronic.

"Hello, Zed," I said. "What have you got for me today?"

"Ah, Number Seven," Zed said with unfeigned enthusiasm. "Here, something for your eyesight."

Zed offered me a pair of Emporio Armani spectacles.

"Sorry Zed, I've twenty twenty vision," I said.

"The glasses are not as they seem."

"Is anything?" I took the glasses.

"Put them on."

I put on the glasses. They fitted perfectly.

Zed produced a calculator from his pocket, and pressed some keys.

I flinched and blinked. The lenses were stereoscopic computer monitors, superimposing a three-dimensional head-up display across my field of vision. The display highlighted Zed with a green reticle, identifying him by name. An assistant on the other side of the room was marked out with a red reticle marking him "unidentified". The device also responded to my eye movement, displaying detailed information about anything at which I looked directly.

"This is a sight for sore eyes," I said. "And what else does it do?"

"Aha," he said as he pressed a couple more buttons on his calculator.

The display changed to infrared, marking out living things from inanimate. The software used an x-ray overlay where appropriate, and I could see that Zed was carrying a concealed weapon in a shoulder holster.

The lenses also displayed menus and tabs, presumably accessed using the calculator.

"It's also got night vision," Zed explained, "and very limited algorithmic precognition, displaying the likely actions of your enemies for the next few seconds. It's not perfect of course."

I scarcely knew what to say. "It's amazing, Zed."

"Not a bit of it." Zed blushed a little. "Just a bit of simple programming. The algorithm's mine, and my boffins wrote the software. It's nothing really."

"Absolutely amazing."

"Not amazing enough, I'm afraid," he said, sighing. "It wreaks havoc with anything electronic."

Televisions and computer monitors all around the room were being interfered with, displaying distorted pictures, issuing white noise.

He switched off the keypad. The display in the glasses disappeared, and the electronics once again worked as they were meant to.

Zed handed me the calculator-like device. I turned it over. There was a warning label—Caution: This device produces electromagnetic interference.

"You've got to get this thing properly shielded."

"Oh yes," Zed huffed, "in my spare time, Number Seven. Anyway, with that little thing you've got access to a large database including images and video on anything relevant to your assignment—and anything that isn't. I hope I can trust you not to waste its capabilities by merely using it to surf the web."

"Thank you, Zed. It should come in very handy. But why a calculator? Why not a mobile phone?"

Zed shrugged. "Call me old-fashioned. Anyway, you never know when you might need to count the cost."

That evening, I found myself seated, first-class, on a jet bound for the familiar territory of the Côte d'Azur.

Zed had suggested I wear the glasses all the time, and I complied.

Extracting the calculator device from my pocket, I punched a few keys. My head-up overlay displayed the dossier on Stephen Gates. There was his picture, well groomed in a shirt and tie, and some additional information about the McGuffin, the robbery, and Gates's likely whereabouts in Monte Carlo.

The glasses also showed me the likely actions of the people around me. Using rudimentary 3-D models of the people in my field of view, it projected a situation of panic and pandemonium as the plane plummeted.

True to the virtual simulation, the aircraft began bucking, and then nosed into an out-of-control dive.

The cabin crew held on for their lives, while the passengers screamed. All the seat-back television monitors began displaying only snowy noise.

My overlay flashed the words "FREE FALL WARNING" in red before my eyes.

I switched the device off.

Within seconds the pilot regained control and we resumed cruising normally, albeit with a few bruised heads and spilled drinks.

"Your crew apologise for the turbulence," a voice said over the ship's tannoy. "May we take this opportunity to remind you that you may only use approved electronic devices. Thank you."

Fair enough. This device could hardly be considered approved.

At the scheduled time the plane landed, and I acquired a luxury rental car at the airport. This vehicle wouldn't have any of Zed's modifications—he didn't use Hertz.

I knew the stretch of road well which skirted the Côte d'Azur, the beach on my right and the hills on my left, and drove it fast.

The bright lights of Monte Carlo sprang from the darkness as I crested a hill.

I drove on, entering the principality by the coastal road to the perfect visibility of the well lit boulevards, making for the casino.

I stopped the car in front of the Hôtel de Paris, the palace of five-star elegance next door to the famous casino. I gave the keys to a valet who was waiting at the entrance to the hotel.

The valet got in the car, started the engine, and launched away with a squeal of tyres.

I entered the hotel reception to check-in, and read the desk clerk's name badge. "Good evening Jules. I have a reservation. My name is Stone. My luggage is in my car, though that might be halfway across Monaco by now."

"Fine Mr Stone. Just sign in, and I'll have you shown to your room."

I signed the guest book. "Just give me the key. I'll be starting in the casino this evening."

"As you wish sir." The clerk gave me a key. "And may I wish you good luck in the casino?"

"Thank you, but there's always a certain amount of skill, discretion, and destiny mixed in."

"Of course," Jules said. "Good luck, nevertheless."

The hotel lobby was adorned with a number of mirrors, and I checked my reflection. My suit was perfect save that my tie needed straightening.

I left the hotel and crossed the plaza to enter the casino.

I entered the atrium, the outer area where tourists and casual players congregated, crowded with people looking for a relatively cheap thrill on the slot machines. The serious players would be at the table games, but I couldn't have said that Gates wouldn't spend any time with the slot machines.

It was hard to see. The crowd was thick and the light was dim. Reaching into my pocket with one hand and adjusting my glasses with the other, I activated the overlay in hope that it could enhance my efforts.

The display flickered into life, superimposing reticles on all the gamblers and basic information about my surroundings.

Next to me, a slot machine rang out its jackpot klaxon. The lucky gambler had won big, flapping her arms and screaming in outrageous excitement while attracting the envious looks of the casino's other patrons.

I walked on.

Another machine rang out, and another punter struck the jackpot, again right next to me, bringing further attention and whoops of delight. I walked a little faster, uncomfortable.

Each machine I passed struck the top prize, wailing a cacophony of bells, electronic bleeps, and euphoric screams. One of the machines that paid out wasn't even in use.

I didn't like how this was going to look on the security camera footage. My licence to kill could allow death and injury to be overlooked, but—to the casino at least—this damage would be far greater.

I switched off my overlay and moved on.

The door to the main gaming salon was flanked by concierges who checked that those entering these hallowed halls were properly dressed.

The cut of my suit granted me immediate entry with no questions.

The elegance of the gaming tables, surrounded by their well-dressed clientele, welcomed me as I surreptitiously patrolled the place looking for Gates and Jessica. I soon found the couple at a roulette table.

The croupier had just spun the wheel and set the ball rolling with the probability of collecting ninety percent of the money on the table. Not if I could help it.

Checking for nearby electronics, I switched my over-lay on again. I heard a few hearing aids and radios squeal. I could live with that. I wondered if Zed's precognitive algorithm would work with the roulette ball.

I held a stack of chips in my hand and watched the targeting reticle follow the orbiting ball. Another reticle appeared, following a number on the wheel, but too fast for me to read it. Keeping my chips poised and ready, I watched until the wheel had slowed enough for me to make out the number.

Zed's gadget was indicating twenty-two.

Hoping his boffins knew their stuff, I trusted my stack to them on twenty-two. My chips were the only ones on that square. The other gamblers had made various bets—black or red, odd or even, some straddling the lines so as to cover two or four options. None of these improve the odds, fixed to favour the house in any combination. Roulette is a game for suckers—unless one has precognition.

"No more bets," the croupier said as the wheel and ball slowed to a predetermined minimum.

The ball bounced into its space on the wheel: twenty-two. Most of the players groaned. Gates showed no emotion.

"Twenty two. Even. Black. Second twelve." The croupier called out the winners, which was only me and my full stack at thirty-seven to one odds.

Apart from my Bentley, Mayfair apartment, and a taste for Bollinger and caviar, my needs were modest. I gambled with company funds, so the company would keep the winnings. Really, Zed deserved them.

I was watching Gates. I guessed he had been losing all evening, while I had only just arrived.

The croupier pushed a large pile of chips to me.

I slid one of the larger chips across the table to the croupier as a gratuity. "Would you please have these sent to the cashier? I'll collect them a little later." The croupier took my chips back to carry out my request.

Jessica smiled at me.

Gates frowned at me as he took Jessica's hand and turned to leave, pushing past me with an an icy shoulder.

"Excuse me," I said, "please don't leave. You enjoy high stakes. I was looking forward to competing with you."

Gates glared, surely wondering who I was and how soon I could be killed. "Perhaps some other time, Mister…"

"Stone," I said. "Donovan Stone." I took the hand he was not offering and shook it.

"But tonight we're exhausted." Gates released a heavy sigh and rubbed his eyes with his free hand, the other of which I still held. "Physically and financially."

I kept Gates's hand a little longer before releasing it. "Good night, then. Or rather good morning. I hope we meet again soon."

I shook Jessica's hand as well, surreptitiously passing her a note.

"That goes for both of you, of course," I said.

"If we do I'll see you get your comeuppance. Good bye Mr Stone." Gates offered me his most threatening half smile.

I afforded him a nonthreatening full smile. And then they were gone.

I left the casino and returned to my hotel to pass the remainder of the night sleeping.

The following day I performed my few official duties before finding other ways to pass the time, generally at the gaming tables, while keeping tabs on Gates and Jessica. In order to keep a low profile I played without the benefit of my new toy. Gambling with a precognitive algorithm isn't gambling—it takes away all the excitement.

Gates spent most of his day in the casino, mostly losing, with Jessica on his arm at all times.

That night I dined alone in the hotel restaurant. The food was outstanding but it was really just a way of passing the time, and I dragged it out as long as necessary.

About eleven o'clock I retreated to the hotel lobby and, tired as though my working day was finished, seated myself at a two-person table and ordered a pot of tea.

I settled down to read a tawdry French espionage novel I had selected at the gift shop.

An hour later, tiring of the exploits of the Gallic spy whose name sounded like a flower, I watched the clock on the wall tick over to midnight.

Jessica appeared at my table. Her nocturnal attire of a loose fitting tracksuit and running shoes took me by surprise, contrasting with the suit I still wore. She glanced over her shoulder, right and left.

I put down my book and stood. "Thank you for taking my note seriously. I wasn't sure you'd come." I moved around the table to hold her chair as she sat down.

"Why did you ask me here?"

"Because there's something about you that I'm drawn to," I said, returning to my seat. "Why did you come?"

She smiled bashfully. "The same, I suppose."

The lounge was maintained at a pleasant temperature. Jessica removed her hooded sweatshirt, revealing an over-size tee shirt with a famous sports logo on the front. I kept my jacket and tie intact.

We chatted for an hour over a fresh pot of tea.

The clock struck one.

Then two.

We passed yet another pleasant hour of conversation.

Three.

Of course, I was manipulating her, trying to follow my orders. Nevertheless, the hours flew.

At some unremembered point I had removed my jacket and draped it the back of my chair, loosened my tie, and rolled my sleeves halfway up.

After those few short hours I was no longer tired, and I felt as if I had known Jessica for years. I hoped my feelings were an accurate gauge of hers. I had little experience with such things, and didn't fully recognise what had hit me yet.

Jessica glanced at the splendid custom Rolex on her wrist, chiming an elegant alarm.

"I'm sorry Donovan, that means it's time to go," she said with a distant look in her eyes. "Steven will be getting up in about twenty minutes, so I've got to go make myself look like I've been sleeping."

At that moment, the barman appeared next to Jessica, holding an ornate antique style phone. "Mademoiselle, a telephone call for you," he said.

Jessica accepted the call. "Yes?" She listened for a moment. "No, thank you." She gave the receiver back to the barkeeper, who took it away.

"Who was that?"

Jessica looked puzzled. "A Mr Ascellis asking me to accompany him to the plaice fisheries' undersea benefit ball and kendo demonstration."

"Strange. Who is this Mr Ascellis?"

"I've never heard of him before. Some kind of prankster I suppose."

Jessica stood, and so did I, picking up our things.

"Can we meet again tonight?" I said, trying to make contact with her averted eyes.

"Only if you'll be in Paris," she said, looking away at nothing specific. "We're flying there this morning."

"For you, I'll be in Paris tonight. Meet me at the Ritz, in the cocktail lounge."

I took her hand as she looked at the floor.

"Midnight?" she asked, hesitantly.

"Midnight," I said.

"All right. Until then…"

Jessica backed away by inches until our hands parted.

She resumed eye contact with me before turning and making for the exit.

I couldn't take my eyes off her until I had no choice. She was gone.

I checked out of my room, retrieved my car, and drove hard all day, making Paris by evening.

The Ritz accepted my booking under my real name, but I paid for my room using my Global Imports expense account.

Around midnight I again found myself seated in the lobby. Same scene, different location.

This time I left my book in my room. I couldn't concentrate enough to read, and I was writing my own story now.

The clock on the wall struck midnight, and Jessica sat down at my table.

"On time as usual," I said, standing for half a second out of conditioned reflex.

"I'm not sure I should have come," Jessica said, her eyes darting into the room's dim corners and alcoves. "Steven noticed that I didn't get any sleep last night. I slept through the entire flight, and had another nap this evening. He's a jealous man, and I wouldn't want you to have to meet him."

"He's also a dangerous man. Jessica, he's not somebody you should be hanging about with. He's mixed up in all sorts of illegal things, and I know that he's brought you into them." I reached across the table and took her hand. "But I also know that you aren't like him. You're gentle and honest and beautiful, but your devotion to him has led you into a darker world, and made you fight for him even though you know it's wrong."

Jessica's eyes were cast down. I could see she was fighting back tears as her lips quivered and her breath quickened.

I inched my chair closer to hers. I put an arm around her to offer some sympathy and—in keeping with my mission—a way out.

"You're right," she said, her voice cracking though no tears flowed. "I've used my abilities for him, when he was involved in some terrible things. Even now..."

She buried her head in my shoulder, her dry eyes leaving no impression there.

"It's all right," I said. "It's never too late to change."

I put my hand under her chin, bringing her eyes up to meet mine.

I gently wiped away her non-existent tears with my thumb.

We peered into each other's eyes for I don't know how many moments.

I brought my lips to hers, kissing her for an instant before she broke away from me in confused distress which might again have brought tears to any other woman.

"I'm sorry, Donovan," Jessica said, her voice cracking and quivering. "This just isn't right. I suppose my feelings for Steven are too strong." I didn't comprehend how evil men could inspire women to such loyalty that they would say it's wrong to leave them. What could be more right than to betray such a man?

"What about your feelings for me?"

"I don't know. I'm confused," Jessica said. She stood up and turned away to avoid my gaze. "I think I should go now."

I stood. "I'll be here tomorrow night, same time."

Jessica returned to her hotel room, messing her hair and removing her make-up before getting into bed.

Later, up and dressed, Gates none too gently woke Jessica up. "Jessica. The day's getting old."

"Uhhh… what time is it?"

"You must be tired, lying in so late. Have you had trouble sleeping?" A snide sneer crossed his lips. "I see that guilty look," he said. "You don't even try to cover it up to avoid hurting my feelings."

Jessica lay motionless and fearful. Gates grabbed her by the wrist, dragging her off the bed and onto the floor. Just as she got her feet under her, he flung her against the wall with a thump. She slid to the floor.

"Who ever he is, I'm better, and I'll prove it if I have to." He advanced on Jessica, standing over her crumpled form. "I'm confident that you'll stay with me."

Gates checked his suit in the mirror and left the room.

Jessica rubbed her bruised wrist for a moment before burying her head in her hands and sobbing.

Throughout the day I kept an eye on Gates and Jessica. It was chilly for the time of year, so I wore my coat and leather gloves.

They breakfasted at the Cafe de Paris on the Champs-Elysées, had lunch at the Restaurant Jules Verne atop the Eiffel Tower, perused some of Paris's better bookshops, and attended the Opera, followed by a return to the Ritz for a late dinner.

Maintaining my discreet distance, I entered the hotel behind them, still cold and unwilling to shed my coat and gloves.

"Monsieur Stone," the clerk on the front desk said. "A letter came for you in today's post."

He held it out to me, and I accepted it, opening it with my gloved hands as I walked toward the dining room.

The letter read, "Mr Ascellis requests the pleasure of your company at the opening of the Slatternly Mews Tea Rooms, which will commence with the auction of the unique Livre des morts des Anciens Luxembourgeois. RSVP to…"

I made a mental note to make a cursory investigation of Mr Ascellis when and if I got home to London.

In the dining room I took a table obscured by en elegant tropical plant as I quit staking out my subjects.

Later that night, as Gates and Jessica lay apparently asleep in bed, Jessica sat up carefully. Gates gave no sign of awareness.

Meanwhile, I waited in the lounge, sipping my tea.

She was ten minutes late.

But I needn't have worried. Jessica took a seat at my table.

"I was afraid," I said, "you might not—"

"Donovan, don't be afraid. I need you to be strong," she said putting her hand on mine and constricting it. "Take me away. Right now."

I smiled to reassure her. "All right."

Jessica and I left the cafe.

Unknown to us, Gates was following us at a discrete distance, appearing as if he'd just got out of bed. He concealed something inside his dressing gown.

I took Jessica's hand. "Do you need anything from your room?"

"No," she said. "Do you?"

"I'll come back for it."

Stopping at the lift, I pressed the call button. The wait, though only a few seconds, was interminable.

The lift opened and we entered.

The doors closed and the lift descended.

After only one floor, the door opened.

Gates was waiting for us, a little out of breath.

Jessica was so startled to see him that she dropped her handbag, which landed at my feet.

I pressed the button to close the door, which began sliding shut, just a trifle too slowly.

Gates opened up his robe, revealing the McGuffin weapon. He raised it and fired a beam at the wall next to the lift door, which penetrated and melted the control panel inside in a shower of sparks, causing the lights to flicker as the electrical supply was interfered with.

The door reopened.

"Hello Jessica. Hello Mr Stone," Gates said, waving at us half-heartedly with his free hand while a demented jealousy burned in his eyes. "I'm afraid, Mr Stone, that I am going to have to use this extremely powerful and technologically advanced weapon on you. It's nothing personal though. Also my dear Jessica, I'm…" Gates's voice cracked with emotion. "That's entirely personal. You see, after this… affair, I know I can't trust you to be faithful to me. And if I can't have you, no one will. The only way to relieve my jealousy is to kill you. And Mr Stone, I must kill you because… well, that's just the way it's done. Good bye."

Wracking my brain to think how I might stop him, it seemed my only option was my pistol. I drew as quickly as I could from my shoulder holster, putting a western gunfighter to shame. But I couldn't compete—Gates's finger was already on his trigger. He fired the McGuffin at my pistol, which glowed red hot. I dropped it on the floor.

My gun hand was seared and in pain, but I couldn't think about it.

Gates was aiming the weapon at me.

But he had trouble firing, hesitating, near to tears.

Using his indecision to my advantage, I kicked Jessica's handbag at him, taking the McGuffin out of his hand.

I jumped on Gates and tackled him to the floor.

Grappling with one another, we wrestled on the tastefully carpeted hotel floor, each of us desperate for the upper hand.

I did my best, but Gates got his feet under me and, with a mighty shove, sent me reeling backward.

I regained my feet and balance, while Gates regained the McGuffin.

"Mr Stone, it appears you really care for Jessica," Gates said, choking back tears and laughing a little at the same time. "Perhaps I shouldn't kill her after all. Maybe I'll sell you her life for a million dollars, and only kill you. What do you think?"

"I don't know," I said, making a slow and deliberate show of reaching into my pocket and removing the calculator. "Let me count the cost."

Gates looked on with interest as I let him see clearly what I was doing.

Getting a firm grip on the device, I poised my finger over the power button, ready to activate it and see what would happen.

I brought my finger down slowly to the device's rubbery button…

Chapter 13 – Truly Out

You are bed-ridden in the intensive care unit at the local hospital, the victim of a deep and critical knife wound. Several machines are wired to you, monitoring, maintaining, transfusing.

One of the machines beeps steadily, indicating no problems with the strong and healthy beating of your heart.

A nurse, a matronly Jamaican woman, stands beside your bed. She rests her hand on yours, willing some life into you.

A doctor reads your charts, monitoring the machines which are monitoring you, and puzzling over your condition with growing concern.

Hudson, dressed in pyjamas and a dressing gown, on his feet but connected to a portable i.v. drip, is engaged in conversation with Dave, who is dressed for his policing duties.

"The Madman," Dave says, "if that's who it was, was gone when we got there. There was quite a bit of blood on the ground, but the dna hasn't identified anyone. Like the van at the ambush scene, this one has somehow slipped through the cracks. A guy like this should have a record."

"Oh, I'm sure it was the Madman," Hudson says. "What have you learned from his crony?"

"Gates? He was unconscious for a long time. The blow to the head he suffered was pretty bad. Well, pretty good. I'm not losing any sleep over his head injury. Anyway, all he's good for is the Madman's physical description, and we got a more detailed one from Don's girlfriend over there," Dave says, pointing to the padded hospital chair in which Jessica sits, dozing under a hospital blanket.

The private room is small, and the six people fill it.

"I wish I could've been there," Hudson says. "I've gotta get out of this place."

"Not much longer," the doctor says, still studying the chart. "At this rate, you'll be home sooner than Mr Stone will."

"Okay," Hudson says. "Not sure if I'd swap places with him or not. I wish he'd wake up, though. What about the jogger? The bag snatcher?"

"He hasn't been seen," Dave says. "He'll be laying low, although nobody got a good enough look at him to identify him." He looks down at you, and then at a newspaper on the chair. "It's funny, but today is the first time Don's got a good write-up in the Oracle."

"Yeah, well, it's not a good write-up for us," Hudson says. "The Madman's back in hiding, and we still don't know who he is or where to find him. We're no closer to finding his protégées either. Unless we can crack the case, someone else is going to get killed. Don was actually being really helpful with that." Hudson turns to the physician. "What's actually his problem, Doc? He looks all right to me."

"It was a simple enough wound. Mainly blood loss." The doctor strokes his stubbly beard in bewilderment. "He should come out of this coma soon, but then, he shouldn't be in it at all. It's probably just concussion. Or something else that we don't know about."

The nurse shakes her head in sympathy and sadness. "I don't know, he was hurt pretty bad. I've seen people die from injuries like he sustained."

"Oh, he's not dying. He's stable. His vitals are strong," the doctor says. "He's obviously got the will to live. But why doesn't he wake up? That I don't know."

If you were awake to hear him you would respect his honesty. But you're not, so you don't.

Chapter 14 – Free Agent

Gates aimed the McGuffin at Jessica, who had trusted me for protection.

My finger was descending to the "on" switch of my calculator-like overlay control.

Gates still hesitated, having the luxury of pressing his advantage.

Knowing Gates wouldn't hesitate forever, I brought my finger down and pressed the button.

The overlay on my glasses booted up, the targeting reticles appearing in green over Gates and in amber over the McGuffin. The reticle changed to red as the device registered the danger that the McGuffin represented.

The precognition feature was loaded into the device's memory and began to operate. It showed a beam firing in our direction, and our bodies falling to the floor. Without doubt, that was the most likely outcome.

But I never believed in fortune-telling.

In defiance of the algorithm's prediction, a shower of sparks flew from the McGuffin like a pyrotechnics display. It made a sound like a firecracker, and the sizzle of electrical discharge as arcs of blue lightning shot up Gates's arm and head.

Gates was jolted to the floor, convulsed by electrical shock. He tried to shake the McGuffin from his hand, but the electricity pouring from the power cell kept his finger muscles contracted tightly around its handle, in the same way that his facial muscles tightened to bare his clenched teeth in a grotesque electric snarl.

It didn't take long for the battery to deplete and the gun to stop arcing and sparking. When it had finished, Gates's inert and lifeless hand relaxed and released the scorched and useless McGuffin. The man himself lay dead on the floor, smoke rising from his marred carcass.

Jessica covered her face with her hands and cried for her lost lover. I dared not guess how long it might take before she would no longer feel his domination and be able to shed the baggage he had left her with.

After giving her a moment to weep alone, I took her into my arms and gave her my shoulder to cry on. This time there were real tears. She was going to be all right.

With the mission over, I was recalled home to London. I would have to make my report, return the damaged McGuffin, and resume my life. Jessica had nowhere else to go, so she came with me. With the seizure of Gates's assets, Jessica had no home, no money, and practically no identity.

Rested, cleaned up, and back to full operating capacity, I stood in front of N's desk. Jessica was seated nearby, looking stunning in a conservative blue suit and hat. N stood behind his desk, a figure of stoical British understatement. An older man I recognised from somewhere stood by me, his hands clasped behind his back, and his tasteful suit giving a hint as to his monetary value.

N leaned across his desk to shake my hand. "Well done, Number Seven. Mission accomplished. The Ministry would like to congratulate you. As I promised, you'll be promoted. We're very impressed with the way you've handled this unusual assignment."

"Thank you, sir."

"No, thank you Number Seven. Now, Walter, I believe you have something to present to Number Seven."

"Yes indeed. Mr Stone, I'm Walter McGuffin, president of McGuffin Electronics. You have been instrumental in saving us millions in revenues by keeping this new weapon away from our competitors. So it gives me great pleasure to present you with this cheque for a percentage of the projected estimated profits. I thank you for your service to us, and to the free world."

Walt handed a cheque to me with his left hand, and offered me his right to shake. I accepted both, and looked at the amount of money that had just been given to me, which was generous, and took it in silently for a moment.

"Thank you both," I said. "But my involvement in this mission has also given me an extra benefit. In fact, Jessica and I have an important announcement to make."

I reached my hand out to Jessica.

"I knew it," belted out Walter McGuffin, clearly thrilled for us. "I just knew it!" He did a peculiar little victory dance, before adding, "I had a feeling about you two!"

Jessica, smiling, rose from her hair chair and took my hand. But she couldn't keep it for a long before N and Walter gave her kisses and hugs and warmly shook my hand. Sherrie and Zed were called in to hear the news, and there were more hugs and handshakes, together with smiles and congratulatory drinks.

Our wedding took place the next day.

As we exited the church as man and wife, we were surrounded by a crowd of people—friends, enemies, and those indifferent—celebrating our day with us. N, Zed, and Sherrie were there, of course. Dave, Bert, Hudson, Arthur, Walter, Dallirama, Zarkov, Murphy, Jimmie—and many others I didn't know, whom I assumed were from Jessica's side—were wishing us well, some smiling, some crying, some smiling and crying, all cheering and throwing so much confetti that it seemed to be snowing a blizzard.

The crowd opened up before us as we walked away from the church, a brisk bounce in our steps. I stopped under the lych gate, pulled Jessica in close, wrapped my arms around her, and gave her a long kiss. The crowd whooped and roared, showering us with rice and confetti, imparting their enthusiasm and affection to us in waves. I kept hold of Jessica, kissing her as if I had waited all my life to do so, as if I couldn't bear to let go of her, which was the truest truth I knew.

But I did let go. We had places to go, things to see, pleasures and pains to share, a life to live together. We ran the gauntlet of friends and well-wishers, clapped on the shoulder, and hand shaken, by other hands too numerous to count. Jessica received with grace and gratitude numerous kisses from our guests.

Then the throng parted before us to reveal my convertible Audi, decorated with its "just married" regalia.

I went round to the passenger side and opened the door for my wife, the new Mrs Stone, the love of my life and my best friend. She got in, pulling in her train and all the straggling tracery of her dress before I closed the door.

Coming around to the driver's side, I noticed a card on the seat. Jessica was picking it up.

I sat down and started the car. The engine roared. A flick of a switch and the top was down, ready for us to enjoy the wind in our hair and the open road.

"Where did this come from?" my bride said.

"Open it and find out," I said.

The tyres squealed as I pressed the accelerator down a little too far and drove the car out onto the coastal highway.

Jessica carefully unsealed the envelope, extracted the card, and opened it. "Who's Mr Ascellis?"

I had forgotten all about him. The card must surely contain some cryptic nonsense masquerading as a greeting. She puzzled over the message.

"Don't read it to me," I said. "I don't want to know."

Jessica obediently stuffed the card in the glovebox.

Mind back on my driving, I raced away at speed, until my wife reminded me that we had all the time in the world.

Slowing the car down to appreciate the coastal setting on the way to our honeymoon and the adventure of life thereafter, we enjoyed the lush green vineyards on our right, the ocean under the red sky and the setting sun on our left.

We fully expected to live happily ever after.

But Mr Ascellis…

"That card," I said. "Does it make any sense?"

"No. It's just gibberish."

I could put it out of my mind. Just tell Jessica to tear it up. I needn't think about it. What did it mean? Why should I have cared?

"Mr Ascellis?" I puzzled over the name.

I snapped my fingers. "Got it! The fingerprint murders. My department tried but failed to catch him. He sent letters which were impregnated to kill only the intended recipient. Last time I got one of his letters I was wearing gloves." But right now I wasn't wearing gloves. They were where gloves should be: in the glove box.

"Then I should get rid of it," Jessica said, removing it from the glovebox and holding it in the air ready for the wind to carry it away.

"No, wait!"

"Why?" Jessica asked.

"It's—" Something about it was important to me. "It's evidence."

"But we're on honeymoon," Jessica said, distressed. "What else does this card mean to you?"

"It means… something."

It meant the resolution to a mystery. A way out of this perfect—oh so perfect—world. It meant an undiscovered country, a messy, unpredictable reign, a point of no return.

"Jessica, it means a decision." I slowed the car, and stopped it at a place where the shoulder was wide enough.

"A decision? What decision? This thing will kill you. It'll take you away from me, and you'll never be able to come back." Her tears fell, as she knew what I was thinking. "Donovan, you have everything you want here, everything you need. Why would you throw it away?"

"It's another world," I said. "And it might need me."

"It can't need you," Jessica sobbed, "like I need you." She held the card out to me in her right hand. She also held out her left hand, showing me the wedding ring I had just put on her finger, offering me a choice between the two. "Please, my love, stay with me."

To my right, the obvious choice. The life of perfect satisfaction, doing what I loved, living with whom I loved. Wasn't that everything I'd always wanted?

And to my left... I didn't even know. Death? A place where Donovan Stone was neither needed nor wanted? A place where he could disappear into quiet oblivion?

"The fact is, I don't know what the card will do. Kill me, without a doubt, but more besides. There's something just out of my reach, something I need to remember. This will give me an answer."

"You want to change all this for the answer to a question you don't even know?" Jessica's tears flowed though she steeled herself to reason with me. "How could it possibly be more important than what we've got? Isn't our marriage all the answer you need?"

Her argument was compelling. Was it really better to leave this world—this oh so perfect world—for... what?

"Yes," I said. "And no. There's somewhere else I belong. I don't want to go there, but this fingerprint poison will take me. The worst part, I don't even know where it 'there' is. I only know that there's something important for me to do, a problem that only I can solve, thanks to Mr Ascellis and his greeting card."

I reached for the card.

Jessica snatched it away. She got out of the car and went to the edge of the road, the other side of which was a cliff over the rocks and the roaring sea below. She held the card out over the windy crags.

I also exited the convertible and went to her.

"But what if you're wrong?" she said, choked with convulsions of despair. "What if the poison just kills you, and you leave me here with a broken heart? Please don't! Please…" Her weeping prevented her saying any more.

A good point. What if I traded everything I ever wanted for death, pure and simple?

"Then I could never forgive myself."

"Don't you joke with me Donovan Stone," she said harshly. "Just stay with me."

I wrapped her in my arms and kissed her.

"You can't make this choice for me, Jessica. It's not in your power. I may never get to say this again, but I love you."

Her tears flowed freely as she looked into my eyes, having no will of her own with which to influence me.

I postponed any further action, giving her a chance to say those words back to me. But she didn't say them.

My choice made, already Jessica's lovely features were becoming indistinct, mannequinlike.

"If there's ever been a time to die, it's now," I said as I lifted my hand and touched Ascellis's card.

Agony, starting in my finger and quickly fanning out, wracked my entire being as the poison got to work.

Blood began to seep out as a wound opened up in my side. I felt dizzy, and the world spun around me. Jessica shifted out of focus, looking increasingly like a shop window dummy, artificial and lifeless.

I floated, rocketing away from the seashore as the world melted away.

Copout

Colours danced across my vision, and a roar dominated my hearing.

Through the psychedelic haze, my body lay, neatly arranged on a hospital bed below my hovering awareness. It breathed its peaceful but tormented respiration as several people watched, oblivious to my levitating consciousness and the unbearable roar that filled my disembodied auditory sense.

Chapter 15 – Life Stroke

Coloured lights dance across your vision, and an indescribable roar fills your ears.

You become aware of things.

Four standing figures are silhouetted by fluorescent ceiling lights.

The figures are speaking to one another. You listen.

Two of the figures are medics—a doctor, and a rather portly black nurse. They are talking quietly about blood loss and stomach injuries. Of the other two figures, one is dressed in a smart suit—you recognise Dave—and the other has five days' growth of beard, dressed in a bathrobe. Hudson!

"Ascellis," you say in little more than a croak.

All four of the figures turn to look at you.

For a moment, nobody moves.

Then, the doctor comes to you, taking your wrist and feeling for your pulse. "Welcome back, Mr Stone."

The nurse smiles a smile which could probably be seen from the back of her head.

"Hey," Dave says, "good to see you back, buddy."

"Buddy?" The word tastes wrong in your mouth as you repeat it back.

"Hi Don," Hudson says. "I'm glad you're not…"

"Dead?" You look at the doctor, nurse, and medical apparatus. "I don't know what happened to me, but I guess it must have been serious."

"I don't know," Hudson says. "What's more serious, a bullet to the gut, or a knife to the gut? What do you think, doc?"

The doctor is busy shining a little light into your eye as he uses his fingers to stop your lids from blinking. "Probably about equal," he says.

As the doctor releases your eyelids, you test your neck muscles, moving your head around and taking in the whole room.

Jessica. She's slumped in a chair and fast asleep.

"What's she doing here?" you say.

Dave reaches out and gently punches Jessica in the shoulder. She opens her bleary eyes and puts her arms in the air, stretching. With a yawn she takes in the new situation. When her eyes meet yours, her joy is palpable.

The nurse replies in her Jamaican accent, "Well, I know it's not visiting hours, but we couldn't very well throw your girlfriend out, could we?"

Girlfriend? The word is strange, and you are about to correct the smiling nurse.

"That's right," Jessica says with a comforting smile. "Unless you've decided to break up with me already." She comes to your side, takes your hand, and looks into your eyes.

"I thought you didn't want me," you say.

"I never said that," Jessica assures you.

You think this over. You feel moisture on your face. Your vision is patchy and blurred. Your chest heaves and convulses. Breathing is difficult. You're lightheaded.

And the nurse's smile is replaced with a frown. "Doctor! The trauma. He's going into shock."

The doctor and the nurse suddenly go into a flap of activity.

"I'm not," you say, despite your sobs and palpitations, "going into shock, you silly woman."

You loop your arm—the arm that does not have an i.v. needle stuck in it—around Jessica's neck and clutch her close to you. As your tears mix with hers she does her best to get an arm around you without disturbing the monitors, wires, and tubes.

After holding each other for you don't know how long, Jessica releases you, and brings her head up a few inches from yours. Another tear falls from her eye before she brings her lips down on yours.

As much as you would like to kiss her forever right now, the tears streaming from your eyes and the sobs that convulse your chest make it awkward.

Jessica stands up, wiping the continuing tears from her eyes with her free hand while she continues to hold yours with the other.

You wipe your eyes as well, needing to wipe away the sobs with the same stroke.

"Hudson. We need to talk," you say as his ears prick up, "about Mr Ascellis."

Hudson looks baffled. "Are you sure you're fully conscious, Don?"

"Are you sure you are? I said, we need to talk about the scallies. They must have written letters to the people on their wish list. After all, what good is a wish list if you don't use it? Those letters must exist, and they've got to be found. Once you've got them, put the crypto boys on them. Those letters are the key to finding out how to contact the scallies, and maybe even the Madman."

"Okay," Hudson says. "I'll get Gregson on it right away."

"We will get these scallies," you say. Nobody responds. "You hear me? We will nail these guys."

"I know you will," Jessica says.

Epilogue

Time moves on regardless. You are beginning to heal.
King Arthur won't admit his mistake, if it was a mistake, and he doesn't re-admit you onto the force. He proceeds as if nothing has changed, with one exception: he back-handedly sanctions your investigation. Two detectives are seconded to your hospital room as "guards".

You and Hudson take full advantage of them as assistants. You have a need for something, they fetch it. You want someone on the wish list interviewed, you send them. And they come through.

Each person on the list has something for you. It's surprising how much these people hold onto. Proper hoarders, the lot. Your guards bring back boxes of correspondence, though they've already sifted out the most relevant items. These letters contain various standards of English, written in various hands. They range from simple enquiries about the recipient's hobbies to invitations to join a militant jihad movement.

None of the letters give a return street address, and communications are always begun with the promise of further communication, which leads to a longer paper trail. Never is there any contact information, though the end of the chain of correspondence always includes an acknowledgement of the recipient's feelings on the subject. For example, "We're sorry you won't be joining us", or something similar.

Cryptographic analysis reveals an encoded e-mail address in one of the letters, as if the sender expected a politician, a captain of industry, or a pillar of the community to have the time or inclination to bother finding and understanding the code. This coded message is of no use to the recipient, but it is of use to you. One point scored against an overenthusiastic wannabe security expert turned wannabe murderer.

The coded e-mail address is actually less useful than the fragments of fingerprints found on the letters and envelopes, which yield further clues.

Apart from sleeping at her grandma's house, Jessica's frequent visits almost make her a resident at the hospital. Her constant eavesdropping on your conversations with Hudson and the guards helps her to learn more about your world. She's more interested than you would have expected. The work is intense, but she makes it a pleasure.

You're into your third day in hospital. The wound is beginning to heal, but some blood still seeps from it from time to time. You might have gone home by now but for that.

When the doctor said he wanted to keep you in for observation he probably hadn't bargained on the ward being made into a temporary police HQ. But he's interested in the investigation too, so he doesn't complain and spends more time with you than with most of his patients.

After a couple of days of analysis, investigation, and perspiration, one of your detective-cum-guards triumphantly enters your room clutching a scrap of paper in his hand which he holds up like a trophy. "We've got 'em," the detective says. "Two addresses."

"You mean our scallies?" you ask, holding your breath.

Hudson, who had been poring over some letters, stands up rapidly before wincing in pain. "Come on, don't keep us in suspense!"

"Of course it's the scallies—I mean, suspects." The detective hands you the scrap of paper.

The names don't mean anything to you, but the addresses do. They are in a none-too-attractive part of town, which was always in accordance with your expectations.

"What are we waiting for then? Let's go and get these scum," Hudson says.

"What are you talking about?" Jessica says. "You've got a forty-five calibre hole in you. You're not going anywhere."

"The doc'll just have to put a cork in it. Plenty of time to rest and recuperate after the perps are caught."

The detective raises his hands to shut Hudson up. "Relax guys. Hudson, if you went you might bleed on the suspects and contaminate any evidence. And Don, you're not even a cop anymore. Anyway, we've already got a team going to get these guys."

Jessica squeezes your hand, smiling. "I told you you'd catch them."

"This isn't me. This is a… a team," you say, putting a sour emphasis on that last word.

"Yes," Jessica says, "and you're part of it. This is not all about you Donovan Stone."

She's right, as usual. Faithful are the wounds of a friend, as usual.

"Don, this was your show," Hudson says. "Without you we never would've got this far. Or at least not this soon. We've got 'em now."

"I'll believe that when the Madman's in custody," you say, frowning.

"I have no doubt," the detective said, "that when you're out of here King Arthur will reinstate you. Maybe even with an apology."

"Now I don't know if I'd believe that, even if I saw it."

You waited. That day they made two arrests. The next day, three.

In all they apprehended ten men, which is how many the evidence suggested there would be.

The Madman, however, left no evidence, no hint as to

his involvement, and certainly no address. And there was no Madman in the phone book.

The next day the doctor discharged you.

You are asleep in your bed, having been home for a full day now.

It's peaceful and dark, the solidly framed movie poster hanging over your head board invisible along with all the other sparse trappings of your bedroom.

The dressing on your wound is fresh, having been replaced before the hospital got rid of you, though a small amount of blood continues to seep into it.

Even now the detectives continue on guard duty, taking residence in your living room, one on the sofa and the other on a li-lo. You told them there was no point, that if the Madman wanted to get you he could easily get past them by stealth or by force.

You were right.

He is ever so patient, entering your room and shutting your bedroom door at a snail's pace and without a sound. The Madman creeps over to your bed unheard and peels away your blankets unfelt. A head-lamp he wears illuminates your sleeping body.

The Madman fastens your wrists to the bar of the head-board just above you with a cable tie, tightly pressing your chunky watch into the bony edge of your wrist.

Being clad only in your boxers because you dislike the extra encumbrance of pyjamas makes Madman's next task easy.

His expert fingers peel the medical tape away from your skin, while he dabs alcohol under the tape with a swab to release the stickiness without giving you a start. After a minute the blood-soiled dressing is discarded on the floor and your wound is exposed.

Using tiny scissors, the Madman snips the surgical thread holding your wounded skin together. The blood begins to seep from the wound more freely while he pulls the fragments of thread away with a pair of tweezers.

At last, the Madman wakes you. "Good morning former police detective Donovan Stone. How'd'ja sleep?"

Your dawning consciousness makes you aware of your wrists, secured to a vertical bar of the headboard by ligatures. By rotating your wrists and dislodging your watch from between them you gain a precious few millimetres of space, helping the circulation in your hands and allowing them to move freely along the shaft to which they're bound.

There is no remaining sleepiness to cloud your vision or your judgement. "I've been expecting you," you say.

"Of course you were," the Madman says. "So were your pals in the lounge."

You grit your teeth. Don't ask. Don't even go there.

"But I've come to visit you," he says, "not them. I've got a special present for you. Thank you for my nose, by the way. I really like it now," he says with a nasal sound.

The Madman produces, from wherever he is keeping his things, a metal box with a clasped lid. He unfastens the clasp and opens the box, causing a sudden rush of cold smoke to slide over the sides of the box and disappear.

His stealthiness abandoned, the Madman extracts a dagger of ice and shows it to you.

Holding the icicle in his bare hand, he brings it to your freshly reopened wound.

You squirm and struggle, making the site of your injury an elusive target for his strange weapon.

The Madman stands to his full height. "Now officer Stone, we can do this the hard way," he says, "or the really hard way."

You try to bring your legs up high enough to get them in front of him for a firm kick. Though it wouldn't exactly free you, it would at least hurt him. But it doesn't work. As soon as you are fully horizontal again the Madman sits his considerable mass down on your pelvic area, pinning your midsection while driving the breath from your lungs.

"We're not going to do this at all," you say in a croak. "You're under arrest. Put down your weapon." Your bold words betray fatigue, fear, and weakness, which the Madman notices.

"I can't hear you detective Stone. I left my hearing aid at home."

He drops the icicle directly into your wound, where it slides home without any resistance.

It comes as no surprise to you that the pain is shattering. The fact that the icicle slides in so easily doesn't seem to help.

"Is it cold?" the Madman says. "Did it feel cold when my knife went into your belly? I got stabbed once, and it felt cold. Maybe it would have been different if the knife was hot." He gently presses the icicle down a little further, and enjoys watching you try to squirm as his weight pins you down.

The Madman continues talking, though you've lost the focus on his words. It's hard to be focused on anything other than the searing agony.

The pain causes your body to convulse, your torso and arms rattling the headboard to its nuts and bolts.

The side-effect of the ice is that it is desensitising your injury, numbing it as effectively as a shot of novocaine. The pain backs off, and you're grateful for the release as the convulsions die down. The Madman looks disappointed. "Hey, I hadn't thought of that. Now, should I find some other way to torment you, or just kill you now?"

"Go on, torment me some more." You pant the words out, still shaking and finding it hard to breathe with his weight pressing on your midsection.

"I like you, Detective. You talk my language."

Though wracked with pain and weakened from your injury, your mind is clear enough to notice the bar to which your hands are bound, and within which is hidden the rolled and now worthless stock certificate.

You wrench the strong metal tube out of its defective moorings and grip it between your manacled wrists, stabbing it directly into the Madman's face. You aim for his eye but miss and slash his cheek instead. The unexpected jab drives him backward a little bit, just out of your reach. The poster above your bed was expensively framed, but not a complete waste of money.

Gaining a bit more play around your wrists when the bar drops away, you compress your hand as best you can and rip it free from the makeshift handcuff. You don't even feel it as it scrapes a layer of skin off the back of your hand. Reaching above your head and grabbing the picture frame with two hands, you smash the poster over the Madman's head.

With the Madman enclosed by the frame, you pull him toward you. He flops down on top of you sideways, his shoulder digging into your sternum and the picture frame splintering around and into both of you.

Allowing him not even an instant to recover, you twist your body and wrap your arms around his neck, finding his trachea with your forearm. You squeeze with all your strength in an attempt to either stop his air supply or break his neck. The Madman resists, flailing his body wildly, grabbing and slashing at you with his fingers and nails. Colours dance before your eyes as your weakened body wants to give up and collapse.

Continuing to thrash like, well, a madman, he rolls you both onto the floor. You damage but don't break an elbow. Your rib isn't as lucky, and the snap is audible. Nevertheless, you maintain your grip even as you go light headed.

You concentrate on retaining consciousness just as much as squeezing the life out of the Madman. He continues to thrash, now beating the back of his head against yours, but you turn your face away and absorb the blows with your skull.

He's not breathing, but he is still moving. That last lungful must have been a good one.

There are no more blows. The Madman ceases his thrashing. He's still trying, and still conscious, but there's not much strength left.

The same goes for you. Your field of vision is filled entirely with phosphenes like a psychedelic laser show, and your awareness of anything other than your grip around the Madman's neck is pretty shaky.

You scream, you shout, use smack your head against your bedside table, anything to stay conscious. The Madman's not dead yet.

But his movement has ceased. He's limp and still. There is, however, still a heartbeat. You can't see or hear, but you can feel it.

You bite your lip until it bleeds, and kick the bed so hard that it painfully breaks your toenail, for that extra shot of adrenaline.

The heartbeat is weakening. No respiration. No movement.

Not good enough.

You suck in a deep breath and hold it while reasserting your grip on the Madman's neck. His heart has stopped. At least, you can't feel it any more. You want to release your grip.

But what if you're wrong? What if his heart and lungs are waiting just to spring back into life as soon as you let go?

Then you will just have to be content to die.

The darkness takes you.

When you come to, the Madman is still lying next to you. He hasn't moved due to the fact that he's still not breathing.

You climb over his lifeless body, and your cuts, bruises, and contusions scream out in pain. The anaesthetic of the ice has faded leaving only torment in its place. That at least reminds you that you're alive.

Every movement of every muscle a hardship, you nevertheless decide that bleeding on the bed will at least be more comfortable than bleeding on the floor.

From your mobile phone on the bedside you call the emergency services. It would take far too much effort to speak, so you just leave the line open.

They'll find you.

No, someone else could find you sooner. You end the call and ring Jessica instead.

It rings—you lose count of how many times after two— and she answers. "Hello Donovan."

You hold the phone to your ear, which hurts.

You try to speak, which hurts even more.

Between your bleeding lip, splintered wood embedded in your skin, concussion, toenail, broken rib, swollen elbow, and bruised sternum, you've forgotten all about the open wound in your abdomen. You can't speak, only moan a bit.

Again, you just leave the line open. She'll know you're in trouble. She'll come, and bring help.

You don't have to speak.

You have the rest of your life to speak to her.

Once more, you succumb to unconsciousness.

When you come to again, Jessica is here, tending your wounds.

You don't know how much time this lasts, but it's not long before paramedics arrive. Soon the police are on the scene as well.

Superintendent Arthur gives you a subdued salute. "You did good, Don."

Jessica holds your hand, radiating her love into you as the ambulance men cart you out.

It's a dream come true.

Thank You For Reading!

Dear Reader,

I hope you enjoyed *Copout*. It is a story I have wanted to tell for a long time. I have a great affection for Donovan and Jessica, and I hope you do too.

While this is the story I wanted to tell, I did not write it just for me. I love feedback. I want to know what you liked, what you loved, even what you hated. I'd love to hear from you. You can connect with me on Facebook. Please like my page and offer some comments, opinions, and questions. My profile name is b.cline.author.

Finally, I need to ask a favour. If you're so inclined, I'd love a review of *Copout*. Loved, hated, or indifferent, I'd just enjoy your feedback. Reviews can be tough to come by these days, and you, the reader, have the power to make or break a book. If you have the time search for me on Amazon, where you can also find my other books.

Thank you so much for reading *Copout* and for spending time with me.

With gratitude,

Bart Cline